Also by Arnold B. Kanter
from Catbird Press

Was That a Tax Lawyer Who Just Flew Over?
The Ins & Outs of Law Firm Mismanagement
Advanced Law Firm Mismanagement

FAIRWEATHER, WINTERS & SOMMERS

Counsellors at Law and Hired Guns

777 East North Boulevard West
Chicago, Illinois 60611
Telephone 312-777-7777
FAX 312-777-7770
Telex 77777
Visa: 777-77-7770 Exp. 7/97

Branch Offices:
Seven Mile Beach,
Grand Cayman Island

Stanley J. Fairweather, Inc.
Oscar E. Winters, P.C.
James Q. Sommers, P.C.
Sherman A. Clayton
Stephen I. Falderall
Rudolph A. Grossbladt
Seymour "Nails"® Nuttree
Manley A. Fairweather
Rex A. Gladhand
Seymour I. Plain
F. Frederick Feedrop
Phillip D. W. Wilson III
Franklin Goodtime
T. William Williams
Herbert Gander
Emanuel E. Candoo
Harold W. Punctillio
Robert P. Mentor
Harold C. Ratchet
Garrison M. Phelps

Vance L. Winkle III
Alphonse Proust
Harvey H. Holdem
Hector A. Morgan
Percifal Snikkety
Ruth T. Tender
Rodriguez Hiram-Betty
Gerald O. Forspiel
Hiram Miltoast
Jane Hokum-Cohen
Susan V. Pritchet
Otto M. Flack
Sylvia C. Wurrier
Lionel N. Hartz
Harriet R. Akers
Rachel B. Steinberg
Geodfrey A. Bleschieu
Fawn Plush
Frederick J. Jones
Lydia L. Milife

Alexander P. Pouts
James S. Freeport
Dolly Fu Lish
Laurence G. Highner
Ellen Jane Ritton
Gary Swath
Arthur Y. Fortran
Rebecca M. Avridge
Stephen B. Mostrow
Lancelot X. Byte
Helen M. Laser
Penelope P. Pincher
Patrick Conshenz
Sheldon I. Horvitz
David Z. Alms
Heather R. Regale
Lydia C. Dos
Henry G. LaPlacca
Beverly Post-Humous

No Longer With Us,
Except in Our Hearts
Fairbut W. Cooler

Stan's Secretary:
Geraldine Oxenhandle

Firm Administrator:
Lt. Colonel Clinton
   Hargraves, CPA

Comptroller:
Orville P. Figuremeister

Recruitment Administrator:
Rose Rusho-Cruter

Of Counsel:
Mrs. Mildred Fairweather

THE HANDBOOK OF
LAW FIRM MISMANAGEMENT

From the Offices of
Fairweather, Winters & Sommers

BY ARNOLD B. KANTER

Illustrated by Paul Hoffman

CATBIRD PRESS

CATBIRD PRESS, 16 Windsor Road, North Haven, CT 06473
800-360-2391, catbird@pipeline.com.
If you like this book and would like to see what else
we publish, please write, call, or E-mail us for our catalog.
Kanter's legal humor books are available at special bulk-purchase
discounts for gifts, promotions, and fund-raising.
For details, contact Catbird Press.

Our books are distributed to the trade
by Independent Publishers Group.

Library of Congress Cataloging-in-Publication Data

Kanter, Arnold B.. 1942-
The handbook of law firm mismanagement :
from the offices of Fairweather, Winters & Sommers /
by Arnold B. Kanter ; illustrated by Paul Hoffman.
ISBN 0-945774-12-5 (pbk.)
1. Lawyers—Humor. I. Title
PS3561.A477H36   1990
818'.5402—dc20   90-39970 CIP

Thanks:

To my wife, Carol, and daughter Jodi, for their invaluable assistance in editing this book; to my daughter Wendy for staying the hell out of the way (and, later, even helping out); to Janie Winkler, for typing the manuscript, many times; to Rob Wechsler for paying me a few bucks to write this thing and for his foresight in recognizing what a hilarious book it would turn out to be (and for his invaluable editorial suggestions); to Susan Sneider for proofreading the manuscript; and to publications such as *Chicago Lawyer, Student Lawyer, The American Dui Association Journal,* and others for keeping the Fairweather, Winters & Sommers firm in business over the years.

ARNOLD B. KANTER is one of eight people in the United States who thinks law firms are a stitch. He developed this belief in a futile attempt to maintain his sanity while practicing law at a big and incredibly prestigious Chicago law firm (now he is a consultant to such firms). Versions of the pieces included in this book appeared in publications around the country, including *Chicago Lawyer, Student Lawyer, The American Bar Association Journal,* and various state and local bar journals.

Arnie now splits his time between his homes on Martha's Vineyard and the French Riviera, writing novels, puffing on a Meerschaum, wearing cardigans and romping along the beaches with his German Shepherd, Spot. Actually, that's a lie. He sits at home in Evanston, Illinois, hoping somebody will fax him (or his cat, Johnson) something important.

PAUL HOFFMAN drew the illustrations in this book to accompany Arnold Kanter's pieces when they originally appeared in *Chicago Lawyer.* He has since illustrated three more books by Kanter and Jeffrey Shaffer's *I'm Right Here, Fish-Cake* for Catbird, as well as several books for such publishers as Workman, Running, Rodale, and Harvard Common. His work has also appeared in such places as the *New York Times* and *Boston Globe.* He lives and draws in Greenfield, Massachusetts.

CONTENTS

Foreword   *ix*

LAW AS A BUSINESS
Introduction   *11*
Next Slide, Please   *12*
Oh Captain, My Captain   *16*
The Future Is Ours   *20*
Hold the Baloney!   *23*
Bertha's Bonanza   *26*
Our Little Corner of the World   *31*
Merger Mania   *35*
Malpractice for Fun and Profit   *39*

ADMINISTRATION
Introduction   *43*
Gripe No More   *43*
A Tidy Mess   *48*
Just the Fax, Please, Ma'am   *52*
Outer Space   *57*
A Firm, By Any Other Name   *61*
Ethics in the Air   *65*
Treated Like Dirt   *69*
Unconscious, But Productive   *74*

RECRUITMENT
Introduction   *79*
This Will Hurt You More Than It Hurts Us   *80*
Summer Romance   *85*
Sommers Camp   *90*
Hiring Wars   *93*
Making Womb for More Lawyers   *96*
It's For Your Own Good   *101*

Slipping Them In, Laterally   *106*
The Associate Draft   *110*

ASSOCIATES

Introduction   *115*
Time Flies   *116*
Turn About Is Fair Play   *121*
Outplacement for Profit   *125*
The Feline Perk   *129*
Undue Process   *134*
You've Gone About As Far As You Can Go, Lex   *137*
Health Makes Wealth   *142*
So Long, It's Been Good T'Know Ya   *146*
Partnership Parody   *150*

PARTNERS

Introduction   *157*
Handbook of Infallibility   *158*
Whom to Anoint?   *163*
Howdy, Pardner   *167*
The Ballad of Nails Nuttree   *172*
Slicing the Partnership Pie   *176*
The Nominations Are Closed   *181*
Ebbing the Partnership Flow   *184*
Off with His Head   *188*
Concluding Note   *192*

FOREWORD

You learn from your mistakes. And no law firm in the world has had greater learning opportunity than Fairweather, Winters & Sommers.

In an effort to help other firms avoid the potholes into which it has skidded (and in an effort to recoup, through royalties, to some small extent, the costs of those mishaps), the Fairweather firm has put together this collection of memos, transcripts of committee and department meetings, and miscellanea. The publisher is extremely pleased to have convinced Stanley J. Fairweather, progenitor of the firm, to write a brief introduction to each section of the book.

Read these offerings carefully. Smile, perhaps. But remember always—there but for the grace of God go you.

LAW AS A BUSINESS

Introduction

Most lawyers went to law school because they didn't have the drive for business, or the stomach for blood. Faced with the need to compete (and often to let some blood), we lawyers ran into some difficult times.

Law used to be a profession, back when I started. We never worried much about marketing our services, financing our receivables, organizing our firm, opening new offices, merging, hiring consultants and so forth. Hell, those were things that *clients* did.

Now, of course, all that has changed. Seems we spend most of our time on business matters. Progress. Marvelous, isn't it?

If I were asked (as I have been) to sum up what I did wrong in managing my firm, I could do it in two words—share power. Democracy is greatly overrated as a way to run a law firm. Give me a benign dictatorship anytime. Especially when I'm the dictator.

Folks were feeling powerless around my firm. So I established committees to try to hide the fact that they *were* powerless. It gave people something to do. Trouble with giving people something to do, though, is that sometimes they do it. And doing it—or the attempt to do it— got us into hot water, as you will see in the pages that follow.

Next Slide, Please

The Executive Committee of Fairweather, Winters & Sommers very nearly found itself in the middle of a good argument Tuesday last. Not that that, in itself, is terribly unusual. A lively spat is generally nestled amidst most every Executive Committee meeting. But this one assumed uncommon importance, because at stake was the very structure of the firm.

To set the stage, flash back to a more or less typical E.C. meeting held some eight months ago. The House Committee, affectionately "Brooms and Mops," was presenting a compost of weighty matters for Executive Committee consideration. Among other things, advice of the E.C. was sought (i) on whether the firm should ditch the Lanier pocket secretary in favor of Norelco's new pocket partner, (ii) on the optimum proportion of decaf coffee that should be stocked, and (iii) on whether mailroom personnel should be required to wear blue jackets. A scant two-and-a-half hours sufficed to dispose of the above issues, save whether mailroom personnel should be required to don blue jackets, which was thought to be of sufficient moment to require action by the full partnership.

As the E.C. meeting drew to a close, Seymour "Nails" Nuttree queried whether there wasn't something wrong with a firm organization that obliged its eleven most productive partners to while away two-and-a-half hours on such trivial issues. After discussing this question for twenty-five minutes, the E.C. voted 5-4 (two members abstaining) that there *was* something wrong with such an organization. Thereupon it was moved that the firm engage a consultant to review and evaluate the firm's present structure and, if necessary, to recommend changes. Conceding Ruth Tender's point that such a study was likely to cost money, a majority of the committee concluded, nonetheless, that it would be worth it.

Tuesday last, at long last, was the meeting at which the view of the majority—that it would be worth it—would be sorely tested. The consulting firm was scheduled to make its report.

Armed with spiffy-looking plastic binders, a personalized copy for each E.C. member, the three consultants were ushered into the board room. Stanley Fairweather introduced Harry Strucksure, the head consultant, a law firm specialist who had spent the better part of the last fifteen years telling law firms what was wrong with them. Prior to hanging out his consultant's shingle, Strucksure had spent eight years counting pencils for a minor accounting firm.

Without further ado, Harry took refuge in the charts he had brought. These, he said, were indispensable to comprehending the consultants' recommendations, providing, as they did, the necessary historical backdrop.

Starting with the simplest of structures—the sole practitioner—Harry began projecting the charts on a screen:

Harry explained that, in this diagram, the sole practitioner was represented by the box on the top and the client by the box at the bottom. One partner thought the sole practitioner looked a little like James Sommers, but Harry said that any likeness was unintentional.

Hearing no questions about this slide, he progressed to the sole practitioner with secretary:

Several partners objected that this slide was sexist, presuming, as it did, a male attorney and a female secretary. But Harry countered that he happened to know this attorney and secretary, that they were, respectively, male and female, and that, therefore, far from being sexist, any contrary depiction would have been libelous.

Grinning triumphantly, Harry flashed the next slide, which showed an office-sharing arrangement:

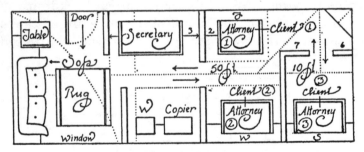

Unfortunately, intermixed with the charts at this point were a few shots of Harry and the family on their recent trip to the Yucatan, which detracted from the professionalism, but added to the interest, of his presentation.

Deflecting additional questions about Chichen Itza, Harry regained his composure and flashed on the screen a simple partnership organization:

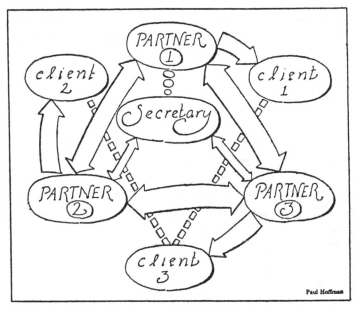

Paul Hoffman

Harry noted (parenthetically) that, viewed correctly, this slide could double as a pool primer, diagramming how client 3, if struck with proper English, could send partner 2 into secretary, who, if she were English, could knock client 1 into the side pocket and, with proper draw, leave client 3 in a position to put client 2 into the left corner.

From this point on, the diagrams got progressively more complex, as Harry flashed slides that approximated the firm's current structure or presented variations that the consultants felt would enhance FWS's operations. Committees, administrators, managing partners and the partnership as a whole jutted out at bizarre angles, depending upon the alternative being presented. Some proposals resembled grotesque Christmas trees, others the DNA molecule; some intricate football plays and others malformed cows with many udders.

Picking up speed as he described alternative after alternative, something appeared suddenly to snap in Harry's organizational center. He burst abruptly into song: "Oh, the Executive Committee's connected to the House Committee. And the House Committee's connected to the Library Committee . . ." to the tune of "Dem Bones." As the E.C. broke into spontaneous applause, his two co-consultants grabbed Harry in a vain attempt to restrain him.

With uncommon strength for a management consultant, Harry broke loose, exited the conference room and railed about the corridors of the firm screeching, "managing partner, Executive Committee, organization must be changed, all wrong, streamline, more power to committees, accountability, power to the people, we shall overcome," until he was at last subdued by two firm employees who arrested his activity by slipping him into a newly ordered blue mailroom jacket—backwards.

Further turmoil was averted when the balance of the consultants' report was deferred until a time very uncertain. And the E.C. turned purposefully to the next item on their agenda—the House Committee's proposal to discontinue decaf coffee.

Oh Captain, My Captain

"I still think we need more facts," said Stephen Falderall, of the Fairweather, Winters & Sommers Executive Committee.

"But we've put this decision over twice already," countered Sue Pritchet.

"But even if we could achieve some cost savings," Falderall protested, "how can we make an intelligent decision on whether to cut out decaf coffee without a survey as to how many cups people drink and how many people in the firm prefer decaf to regular?"

"Look, the House Committee projects that we could save over $700 a year by concentrating all of our purchases on regular coffee and buying in quantity," argued Pritchet.

"You look; for over three meetings seven members of our Executive Committee have considered this issue for a total of at least an hour and a half," said Falderall. "If you figure an average billing rate of $150 an hour, we've already spent $1775 in deciding whether we can save $700."

"I missed one of those meetings," objected Harry Punctillio.

"I think what we need is a more efficient way of handling these kinds of decisions," offered Jane Hokum-Cohen. "Didn't those management consultants we hired suggest we consider a managing partner?"

"But we've never had a managing partner before," Punctillio protested.

"Well, there was a time when we didn't have an Executive Committee either, Harry. Times change," offered Falderall.

"No Executive Committee. When?"

"A long time ago, Harry; in the time of the kings, the reign of Mayor Daley I."

"Assuming arguendo that we did have a managing partner," interrupted Hokum-Cohen, "what would we call him?"

"Wouldn't that depend on his name?" asked Harry. "Or her name; it could be a her, too."

"No, I mean what title. 'Managing partner' sounds a bit too strong. I mean won't we, the Executive Committee, still be 'managing'?"

"I suppose," said Pritchet. "How about 'chief executive officer'?"

"Too corporate," Robert Mentor interjected. "I'd go for something like 'administrative partner.' "

"Too menial," Falderall objected.

"Look, why don't we try to decide what this person would do. Then maybe we could come up with an appropriate title," suggested Sue.

"Fabulous idea, Sue," said Harry. "For starters, this person could decide whether to do away with decaf coffee."

"All alone? Wouldn't he need the advice and consent of the Executive Committee?" asked Hokum-Cohen.

"No. I say if we're going this route, let's bite the bullet," Harry opined.

"What about things like partnership share? Would the managing partner have control over that?" asked Falderall.

"You must be on some kinda dope. Can you imagine the partnership turning that over to one person?" asked Pritchet.

"We do now. Stanley Fairweather decides all of that," Nails reminded the group.

"Sure, but that's different, that's Stanley. We're talking about a managing partner," Pritchet replied.

"What would the term of this person be?" asked Nails.

"Two-and-a-half years," answered Mentor.

"Where did you get that from?" asked Jane.

"Well, it's between two and three, and it seemed not too long and not too short," replied Mentor.

"Let's put that aside for a minute," said Falderall. "Are we anticipating that the person who assumes this position would have to give up his practice?"

"Not entirely," said Pritchet, "but he'd probably have to cut back quite a bit."

"Two-thirds," offered Mentor.

"Between three-fourths and a half, Robert?" asked Jane.

"You catch on quick," said Robert.

"That would be pretty tough," Nails commented. "Do you think we could get somebody who would be willing to do that?"

"I think we could; it would be a pretty prestigious position," offered Mentor.

"Why, because of the complete control over coffee

decisions? Hell, I let my husband do that at home," Sue said. "And it doesn't seem to have gone to his head."

"What type of person are we looking for to fill the position?" queried Mentor.

"Has to be intelligent," said Sue.

"I'd say he'd need good judgment and would have to be even-handed," added Hokum-Cohen.

"And don't forget tact—and humility," offered Falderall.

"Damn, we'd better start looking outside the firm," Harry opined.

The meeting continued for another hour, without noticeable progress. So as not to leave the meeting without some agreement on the managing partner issue, though, the committee voted unanimously to adopt Robert Mentor's suggestion that the managing partner, if one were to be selected, and whatever his title and whatever his duties might be, would serve a two-and-a-half-year term.

And, on Pritchet's motion, the decision as to whether to do away with decaf coffee was tabled until the next meeting, or until the election of a managing partner, whichever occurred first.

The Future Is Ours

The one committee at Fairweather, Winters & Sommers
for whom the question "Is there any new business?" is more
than a platitude is the Committee on New Business.

The committee was formed some years ago at a session
of the Long-Range Planning Committee, chaired by Herbert
Gander. Here is how it all came about.

The Long-Range Planning Committee met in a weekend
retreat session at the Moosetoe Lodge on the outskirts
of a little town not far away from another village not far
away from another little town. Members of the committee
were given detailed directions on how to get to the lodge
by Herbert Gander, himself a founding Moosetoe. The
meeting was delayed a day when five of the seven committee members phoned the lodge to say that they had
followed Herb's directions and they had all wound up at
the same Holiday Inn, some 240 miles from the Moosetoe.

When the throng had finally arrived, Herb suggested
that the committee focus its attention on what the firm
would need if it were to be in existence say ten or fifteen
years from now. Hiram Miltoast offered that they would
certainly need a supply of legal pads. Though electronics
was taking over the place, he could not see the legal pad
disappearing within the decade. But Helen Laser thought
that stockpiling legal pads for the next ten or fifteen years
was not what the people who created the Long-Range
Planning Committee had had in mind as its function.

Sheldon Horvitz thought that for the firm to be in
existence, the world would have to be a different place,
and therefore suggested that the firm start a Committee
on Disarmament. The committee tabled the suggestion,
opting to give the superpowers a tad more time to see
what kind of progress they could make.

"We are going to need the ability to change with the

times," said Hiram Miltoast. "We know the law is going to change, but we don't know *how* it will change. New laws will be passed and old laws will be repealed. Cases will be overruled and cases will be followed. Some will be distinguished and some will be cited as authority for another proposition altogether. New areas of the law will emerge, though hopefully nothing as boring as ERISA—but who knows for sure? The point is that if our firm is to survive, we've got to roll with the punches, to ride the waves, to bend but not break, to be big enough to admit our mistakes—because two wrongs don't make a right—but not so big that we can't see our mistakes because they're too tiny. Nobody is going to do it for us, we've got to walk that lonely valley by ourselves and climb every mountain. I, for one, don't favor hiding this from our partners. I think we ought to come right out and say it to them."

The Chair thanked Hiram for his remarks and motioned to the bartender not to serve him any more drinks.

Harriet Akers said she was concerned about what work the firm would have ten or fifteen years from now. "I don't think that we can assume there is going to be work here ten or fifteen years from now just because there happens to be work here today. Hell, even some of our largest class action suits may be over by then. We have got to be thinking of where our work will be coming from."

James Freeport agreed with Harriet Akers, saying, "I agree with Harriet Akers."

Harriet thanked James Freeport for agreeing with her, noting that she often agreed with what James said, too.

The Chair agreed with both Harriet and James, but said that, to him, the question was how we could assure that there would be work for the firm fifteen years from now.

James said that the key was to attract new clients, and that he had a few ideas as to how to attract them. "Clients are, after all, just people with money who don't pay bills and so should be able to be attracted by means similar to the way other people are attracted. We ought to get a chemist to work on developing a cologne that would attract clients. Since many of them seem to smoke smelly cigars, perhaps some sort of essence of cigar smoke would work. We might also start work on some type of call that they would respond to like 'suee suee,' though that might attract only defendants. Of course, there is also the possibility of a creative advertising campaign offering specials for the month and using a catchy new firm jingle, as our public relations firm, Keepum Fortha Public, has suggested. But I think that we should just start a Committee on New Clients."

Harriet said that, unfortunately, she had to disagree with James this time, though, as she'd said earlier, often she agreed with him. "There isn't a firm in the country that isn't thinking about how to court new clients to get business for the firm, both short and long term. Our committee is supposed to be a creative one, seeking new solutions to problems. We all know that the reason we liked law school so much was that we didn't have to deal with clients. We should see whether we can come up with a way of returning to that blissful state of innocence: clientlessness. Our new committee ought to be called the Committee on New Business, not the Committee on New Clients. If we dream up a way to create business without clients, think what it will do for our recruiting efforts."

The Committee on New Business is still working on the problem.

Hold the Baloney!

The Finance Committee at Fairweather, Winters & Sommers is composed of the seven most financially sophisticated partners in the firm. Below is a report of a recent meeting.

The first order of business was to settle up the luncheon bill from the Mahzel Deli. This exercise was necessitated by the persistent refusal of that bistro to enclose separate checks for lunch orders and complicated by the fact that the author of the check was apparently a would-be doctor whose handwriting, though not his intellect, was Hippocratic. Unable to distinguish meaningfully, on either the paper or the paper plate, between a BLT and a corned beef on rye, Chairman F. Fred Feedrop suggested that each person pony up what he thought to be his fair share.

A tote of these donations drew up $4.23 short and, when each partner plucked out his offering, the last two pluckers found insufficient funds left to cover their initial contributions.

On motion duly made and seconded, each partner restored his original estimate to the kitty, but the retote pulled up $6.45 lame of the Mahzel bill.

The Chairman, recognizing a need for expert guidance, summoned Figuremeister, the firm comptroller, who hazarded that the matter might be entombed if each person chipped in *pro rata* in accordance with his partnership percentage to make up the shortfall. After protracted debate over whether this proposed solution was fair, and what "fair" means anyway, it was concluded, 4-3, that it was not "fair," but the proposal was adopted anyway, with the admonition that the firm once again beseech the Mahzel Deli to render individual checks or at least to engage an inkslinger with a decipherable hand to prepare the tabs.

The committee turned anon to the firm's finances. Copies of the computer print-out of accounts receivable were distributed. Responding to a question from the floor by committee member Gary Swath, who was down there temporarily to reassemble his fallen pastrami sandwich, the Chairman explained what an account receivable was, and pointed out that the print-out showed receivables to be up $500,000 over last year's level.

Sizing up the situation promptly and succinctly, Hector Morgan commented, "So?" James Freeport indicated that, while he did not necessarily disagree with the preceding remark, he regarded the receivables increase as a bad omen. The Chairman quickly whistled the speaker out of order for dealing in the occult.

There followed a period of heated debate over whether the increase in receivables was a good thing or, something quite the opposite, a bad thing. "It's a good thing," argued one. "A bad," insisted another, "No, good," averred a third; "No, bad," a fourth objected. And so on and so forth, getting ever more caustic and witty. Tempers flared, dander rose, tops were blown and handles flew off. But betimes, tranquility restored, Harvey Holdem reasoned that the increase would be a good thing if it bespoke a general increase in hours billed. But a check of the computer print-out of hours billed showed, alack, that they had dipped.

Yet Lionel Hartz ventured his opinion that there was no reason to knit our brows over the increase in dollar amount since, after all, "It is not the amount of the receivables that is important, but their aging." This comment drew a sharp retort from James Sommers, who was long of tooth and thick of ear, to the effect that the utterer of the last remark was not getting any younger himself. The incipient brawl was mooted, however, when an examination of the computer print-out of receivables aging revealed a greater percentage of accounts in the "over 180 days" category than ever before.

By now, even the most optimistic were beginning to feel that the increase in receivables augured ill. The discussion veered next to the general question, "What to do?" Swath evoked a momentary spark of hope when he announced he'd devised an innovative approach to raise funds. While it was true, he admitted, that receivables had risen significantly, payables had skyrocketed even further. The firm had often turned to its bank to finance receivables, but had never considered asking the bank to finance its payables. Just as the committee was about to phone the bank, the Chairman noted a flaw in the financing scheme, pointing out that the firm's payables would provide the bank little security.

At this point, Fawn Plush proposed that the committee hack at the very root of the problem: eliminate the computer print-outs. In its golden days, the firm had no print-outs, never fretted over the things the committee was now discussing, and yet everything turned out both hunky and dory. But we could not simply scotch the computer print-outs, Lionel pointed out, since we were bound, *ex contractu*, to receive them for the next twenty years. Receive them, yes, but that didn't mean we had to look at them, Fawn observed.

At this realization, it was as if a thousand doves had flown at once from our conference room (which, to many, explained why it had begun to get a bit stuffy in there, and rather full of dove droppings). In a transport of delight, the committee readily acceded to Holdem's suggestion that the balance of the receivables matter be resolved by referring it to our comptroller "for action consistent with the sense of this meeting."

While the committee had not exhausted its agenda, it had exhausted its members. Weary but exhilarated over their resolution of the knotty receivables problem, the committee members formed a circle, clasped hands, swayed left and right, and began to chant the traditional

Finance Committee closing prayer, their collective mantra: "Umm, ummmm, ummmmm, ummmmmm. Bott, bott, bott. Bott-ummmm, bot-ummmm, bott-ummmmmm, Bott, ummm-lie, Bott-ummmm-lie, Bott-ummmmmm-lie, bottummmmmmm-line."

Bertha's Bonanza

Few things touch the hearts of FWS partners as much as their stomachs. In fact, filling their stomachs is the preoccupation of one of the most important FWS committees, the Finance Committee.

By "filling their stomachs," of course, one must understand that "stomach" is used figuratively. Used in this sense, it may mean anything from being in a position to afford that second Mercedes, to not having to scrimp on that four-week 'round-the-world vacation, to being able to scrape up the cash for the Jackson Pollock that would just top off the living room refurbishing.

It was matters such as these that formed the backdrop for a recent Finance Committee meeting. Because past meetings had been consumed largely in trying to divide equitably the luncheon bill from Mahzel Deli, the committee, by a 5-2 vote, had determined at its last meeting that each committee member would be required to bring his or her own lunch.

Committee member Morgan did not care for the salami sandwich that his wife had packed and had nearly arranged an even-up swap with Fawn Plush, who was similarly displeased with the peanut butter and jelly that her spouse had tucked into her lunch pail, until the latter discovered that the salami was not on rye. Being a good sport and feeling somewhat that she had committed to do the deal, she swapped Morgan, half for half.

Similar deals were worked out over dessert, with one of the more imaginative being Lionel Hartz's swap of a fudge brownie for a small clump of James Freeport's grapes plus half of James's sandwich at the next meeting.

After lunch the committee members, at the direction of their chairman, tidied up the conference room, and Figuremeister, the firm comptroller, presented a summary of the results of operations for the last fiscal quarter. This showed that, while gross income was up some 14 percent, net income was down 18 percent. In response to a question from Hector Morgan, Figuremeister said that, yes, this would mean that partners would make less money than they did last year. Displeasure spread like wildfire at this news, with comments like "oh heck" and "nuts" being not uncommon.

Fawn asked whether there was a reason for this drop in profitability. Figuremeister said that, yes, there definitely was a reason for this.

Fawn asked if Figuremeister would tell the committee what the reason for the drop was, to which Figuremeister replied, "Sure, why not, that's what you pay me for." The reason for declining profitability, he advised, was a dramatic increase in expenses.

Profitability could be restored either through a reduction of expenses or through an increase in revenues, or through some combination of the two. Balance sheets were passed around to committee members, and Lionel Hartz's hand shot up immediately. "It's clear to me how to solve this problem," he said. "The biggest item of expenditures is associate salaries. It's these little boys and girls who are running home with the bacon while our cupboards are bare. All we have to do is can half of the associates and our net for the three months would have been up 32 percent, and that's not even taking into account what the reduced number of associates would allow us to do in reducing such other major expense items as rent and secretarial costs."

There was a great murmur of approval until Figuremeister pointed out that firing the associates would also have the effect of drastically reducing revenues, since the fired associates could not fairly be expected to continue to bill clients at the same dizzying rate that they had prior to their dismissal.

Water having thus been thrown on what at first blush had seemed a simple solution to the firm's economic woes, the discussion turned to other alternatives for reducing expenses. Hector Morgan pointed out that the firm had, for years, been footing the bill for coffee for both attorneys and staff.

While that might have made sense, he said, when coffee was dirt cheap, it did not seem to him to be necessary in these tough economic times.

Harvey Holdem pointed out that charging for coffee would save each partner a net of only $82 per year, and was likely to produce revolution. Furthermore, the cost of collecting for coffee would probably equal or exceed the revenues to be derived.

A vote was taken on the question of whether free coffee service should be disbanded, and it resulted in a 3-3 tie, with one abstaining. Fawn Plush, a proponent of keeping the free coffee, pointed out that Stanley Fairweather was a six-cup-a-day man and would not be partial to the notion of having to ante up each time he drank. A revote resulted in a 7-0 tally in favor of retaining the free coffee.

Consideration was given to how additional revenue could be raised. Morgan asked whether there weren't other costs that could be passed on to the client without raising legal fees. It always looked better to the client to be reimbursing the firm for expenses, rather than shelling out extra legal fees.

The Chairman agreed with the principle, but questioned whether there were other items left. The firm had been in the forefront of passers-on and had been quite imaginative in laying off on clients the cost of photocopying, word processing, long-distance phone calls, faxing, overtime secretarial help, and messenger services. Somehow, the notion of allocating the cost of pencils, pens and paper to particular clients seemed a tad on the chintzy side.

Gary Swath pointed out that one of the reasons the firm was not more profitable was that clients were taking forever to pay their bills. They were encouraged to do this because their other creditors charged them interest, but FWS did not. Why not add an interest charge to bills, or allow the use of one of the recognized charge cards to pay bills? The firm might even come up with its own credit card: the Fairweather Express Card. With a catchy slogan like, "Charge Your Will and Spread the Bill," it could become a big hit.

Fawn pointed out that any such scheme would require compliance with federal and state truth-in-lending laws. "With all those rules about annual percentage rate and financing charges, I doubt that anyone around here would be able to understand it; we'd have to hire outside counsel," she said. In view of all the complications, the matter was referred to the Long-Range Planning Committee for further consideration and eventual death, the course run by most ideas sent to that body.

The next alternative considered was an across-the-board hike in legal fees. This suggestion was greeted with a level of enthusiasm ranging from strong opposition to threats to resign from the firm. Lionel Hartz pointed out that the firm had already had across-the-board fee increases in two out of the last three quarters, the last of which resulted in one client pointing out that the increase in FWS legal fees had now outstripped the rate of real estate price increases in California. The remark could have been dismissed as a jest had the client not made it to a *Wall Street Journal* reporter who, unfortunately, had the poor taste to print the article, naming FWS.

Gary Swath, one of the freer thinkers in the crowd, suggested that it might be time to start considering going into other lines of business. After extensive discussion, though, the suggestion was dismissed as too progressive for the firm.

A pall was beginning to fall on the assembled throng. The outlook, as 'tis sometimes said, wasn't brilliant. Suggestion after suggestion had been rejected. Tears were beginning to trickle down the cheeks of some of the more vulnerable of the committee members. Remarks like "Bertha's going to kill me when I tell her that she's going to have to get the small Mercedes as a shopping car; I promised her the big one," filled the conference room.

Just then, Stanley Fairweather happened into the room. Sensing from the widespread whimpering that all was not peaches and cream with one of his favorite committees, Stan inquired what the matter might be.

Chairman Feedrop, feeling that as the chief of the committee the responsibility of breaking the news to Stanley was his, said, "Stanley, it's the net. The net is down. And, and, and . . . we, we don't know what to do about it."

"Now, now, now. It's not that bad. Stanley has a little surprise for his Finance Committee." And with this, Stan pulled a check from his pocket. "This little check just came in the mail today as a result of our fees in the Roundup International hostile takeover defense. With it, I think you will find that we are well ahead of last year's figures."

The group burst into spontaneous applause and began singing "For he's a jolly good fellow! . . ."

And from the back of the room a voice said, "God bless you, Stanley J. Fairweather. My Bertha will be so happy."

Our Little Corner of the World

Stanley J. Fairweather, away on his annual vacation in the
Cayman Islands, sent this postcard back to his cohorts:

My Dearest Firm,
I greet you from the sunny Caribbean.
All is not well. The weather is hot. The air con-
ditioner in our condo has been erratic. And the ceiling
fans, while quaint and tropical, blow Mrs. F's hair (would
that I had some to blow) around something awful, and
make a terrible racket besides.

The pool is loaded with children—mainly grand-
children, I think—and I fear that the warmth of the pool
water is not altogether attributable to the sun. The kids
are mean. None of them will give me a turn on their inner
tubes or rafts, and they seem never to shut up, rather like
some of you in committee meetings. And speaking of committee meetings, cancel them until I get back. There is
nothing that can't wait.

I have found lying around the beach to be very con-
ducive to thinking about legal problems. In fact, I am considering redoing the office in a Caribbean motif in order
to increase office productivity. Have the interior designer
sketch out a few alternatives for me to consider when I
return.

In the meantime, I want the guys from the mailroom
to remove the oriental rug and rolltop desk from my office
and haul in four tons of sand, with assorted cigarette
butts. Also, have the bulbs in my chandelier replaced with
sun lamps. And I think it's worth investing a little time
in a training program to teach the messengers to bring in
the office mail and coffee with a calypso beat (you know,

"Day-o issa day, issa day, issa day-ay-ay-o"). If we are going to do it, let's do it right.

I'm afraid that a lot of my best ideas on this trip may be in peril of getting lost forever. I brought one of those new-fangled pocket dictators along, but I forgot the damn tapes. Please ship Ms. Oxenhandle down, quickest way.

I have been giving some preliminary thought to our establishing a branch office down here. While the lack of clients is something of a drawback, the idea has some compensating features which, for tax fraud reasons, I won't delve into here. Trust me.

And I'm working on an idea to improve the client situation and develop a new profit center for the firm at the same time. The problem with the people running the other large law firms today is they're too stodgy to give a bold, new concept a try. Mrs. F and I are taking turns manning the pilot lemonade stand that we set up under a large umbrella on the beach near our condo. This has put us in close touch with lots of potential clients, since our competitive prices and friendly services have attracted huge crowds to the "Fairweather Oasis."

The pilot has proved such a success that we have franchised three oases on other parts of the island, all of which seem to be prospering as well. This may be due to the catchy jingle we are running on local radio:

> You deserve a break today,
> So get up and get away
> To the Fairweather Oases.
> We do it all for you-oo-oo.

We are thinking of adding the "Big Stan," a double turtleburger with trimmings, to the menu. Future promos may feature discounts on simple wills with the purchase of a Big Stan and an Oasis Shake.

Suffice it to say, I've opened the branch office. Remind me to have the Executive Committee ratify this when I get back.

In the meantime, you may want to pick up a copy of the April issue of *The All-American Lawyer*, which is running a nice little feature on me and our new Cayman office entitled "Fairweather Says It's Sink or Swim in the Caymans," complete with photos of yours truly in scuba gear. While the reporter, Sheila Stowaway, was gracious enough to refer to me as "the majestic eagle ray in a school of guppies who dwell around his legal reef," I don't think that she was intending to put any of you down personally. Ms. Stowaway seemed genuinely to enjoy the fortnight that she spent with me and Mrs. F at the condo while writing her piece, and she fairly gushed over the black coral necklace we gave her as a little remembrance, on her last night.

Please express mail two or three associates, a couple of paralegals, an assortment of secretaries and a receptionist to staff our office, pronto. I say pronto because I see death as one of the prime growth areas. And, frankly, there are several of my new buddies down here who, even with their gorgeous tans, don't figure to celebrate too many more Lincoln's Birthdays . . . I mean Presidents' Days.

Last Thursday it was overcast for several hours, so I dropped in on the local law school to try to scare up some potential fodder for the home office. What a pleasure to speak to students who, not having become accustomed to fealty, treat the twenty-minute interview as a chat among equals, rather than the grant of an audience to their potential employer. This may come from the island being too small for employers to fly students from coast to coast.

In candor, though, I am not having the type of success recruiting-wise that I had hoped for, in part because it is not easy to pooh-pooh convincingly a 165-degree temperature difference (even though I've argued vigorously and, to my mind, persuasively, that the windchill factor on Michigan Avenue skews the figures badly). I have, however, made headway in explaining away our sweatshop image as attributable to air-conditioning failure, and I suggest that we may want to waltz that line 'round the law schools, stateside.

Unfortunately, however, even the top students down here may not be of great use to us. They seem to be preoccupied with questions that are of only tangential relevance to those of us north of Cuba, such as whether a dive-boat operator is liable in tort for leading a dive group into a strike of hungry barracuda. And even though the *Cayman Journal of Transoceanic Treasure Trove* is the mothership of the TTT journal fleet, experience on it may not make a student a shoo-in for success in our practice.

With so much time on one's hands down here, there is an opportunity to reflect, to be somewhat more introspective. I have used part of this time to ponder matters such as firm structure and governance. Having ruled the firm with an iron, but tender, fist for the last quarter century, it has occurred to me, as I'm sure it must have occurred, at least in passing, to some of you from time to time, that it might be the hour to pass the torch to a younger generation.

On reflection, however, that seems to me absurd. There isn't anybody around even remotely as gifted as I in running the firm. So, for those of you who dreamt that this might be your big chance, forget it.

I've gotta run now. Even though I print quite small, there is not much room left on this postcard. The day is drawing to a close. Time to shut down the Fairweather Oasis, run up to the condo to shower, fix a piña colada and watch the sun set on the gently heaving ocean.

Wish you all could be here. But you're not. And I am. So eat your hearts out.

Stanley

Merger Mania

A special meeting of the Fairweather Winters & Sommers Long-Range Planning Committee convened on Saturday, May 14th at the Moosetoe Lodge. Because of the sensitive nature of the subject matter, committee members voted to meet behind closed doors, rather than in the bar area of the lodge, as was their wont.

Committee Chair Herbert Gander started: "As we all know, the purpose of this special meeting is to consider whether FWS should merge with another law firm."

Hiram Miltoast said he disagreed.

Gander asked Miltoast how he could disagree; the Executive Committee had charged them with considering the merger question. The Chair misunderstood, Miltoast replied. He did not disagree that the purpose of the meeting was to discuss mergers, only that everyone knew that that was the purpose. "For example," said Miltoast, "I didn't."

Gander thanked Hiram for setting the record straight. Miltoast told Gander not to mention it.

"I wonder whether 'merger' is really what we mean, or whether, perhaps, we may be limiting the scope of our inquiry unduly," wondered Sylvia Wurrier, a corporate specialist. "What about the possibility, for example, of a consolidation or an acquisition?"

Helen Laser, of the tax department, said that she would greatly prefer a 332(q)(3)(AA)(vi)(R2D2)(ii) tax-free exchange to a merger, since that was one of her favorite sections of the Internal Revenue Code. Gander said that he would support anything that could be accomplished without taxes.

Sheldon Horvitz interrupted, saying that if his recollection of his undergraduate philosophy course was correct, the merger notion presented difficult moral and philosophical problems. As he understood it, the firm would completely cease to exist after the merger. "How could we condone that happening to fellow lawyers?" he asked. "And whither would they go?"

Helen Laser tried to explain to Sheldon that, while the firm would cease to exist, the individual members of the firm would continue. Horvitz called that a contradiction in terms and accused Laser of trying to dupe him into believing that the whole could disappear but the parts remain, which he claimed was anti-Hegelian.

Frustrated at the committee's lack of concern over his philosophical point, Horvitz announced: "I'm leaving the meeting. I didn't sit through sit-ins in Selma, teach teach-ins against the Vietnam War and march for the Equal Rights Amendment just to be ignored by a Long-Range Planning Committee."

Harriet Akers suggested it would be easier to consider the question if they listed the advantages and disadvantages of a merger. One person could take the pro-merger side and another the anti-merger side. The rest of the committee could act as a jury. Helen Laser volunteered to take the pro side. Arthur Fortran said he'd argue the con since, although he had not yet decided whether he favored the proposal, he invariably took the opposite side from Helen.

"A merger of our firm with another would make us a larger firm," said Helen, firing the first shot.

"Bigger is not necessarily better," Arthur retorted, smugly. "Besides," he continued, taking the offensive, "having more lawyers would intensify our space problems. And even if we could find sufficient space, how would we arrange the offices? Would they be arranged alternately, one old firm member and then one new firm member? Or boy, girl, boy, girl—or what?"

"So big deal," countered Helen.

"That's not a reply," Arthur complained.

"You blockhead," answered Helen.

Gander interrupted and cautioned Helen to adhere more closely to the subject of the dispute and to lay off of *ad hominem* attacks on Fortran.

"Merging with another firm could give us expertise in areas of practice that we are currently weak in," argued Helen.

"If we've done nicely without them until now, I don't see why we can't continue to do so. More areas of expertise just means more ways to get sued for malpractice," said Arthur. "And having more people around here is just going to make personnel problems worse. We don't get along with each other now. After a merger, there will be more of us not to get along with."

Harriet Akers asked whether there were any actual potential mergers, since it is easier to consider the question in the context of a particular proposal, rather than in the abstract. When the Chair replied that there were no merger proposals, Harriet suggested further discussion be tabled until such time as a proposal was before the committee.

The Chair said that herein lay a problem. In the absence of a specific merger partner, it was indeed difficult to consider the question of whether the firm should merge. However, when a particular merger partner appeared, the matter would no longer be long range but, rather, imminent. At that point, it would be outside of the committee's jurisdiction. In other words, for something to be properly before the committee, it had to be so vague and indefinite as to be incapable of consideration. This, he thought, might go part way towards explaining why lawyers at the firm were not exactly clawing to get onto their committee.

The Chair's remark cast a temporary pall over the meeting. Then Helen suggested a way out of their conundrum. There was no jurisdictional prohibition, she said, to considering hypothetical mergers. If they considered the desirability of a merger under a variety of assumptions, they'd be prepared in the event that one of them became an actual possibility.

Chairman Gander pointed out, though, that there were an unlimited number of variable situations that might prevail in a real merger, and each situation would require a different analysis. It would thus be a poor use of the committee's valuable time to consider hypothetical mergers.

Gander did have another suggestion, however. The committee could develop a list of conditions that would have to be met before the firm would even consider a merger. In this way, the firm could save time by eliminating, right off, any merger that did not meet the threshold criteria.

Delighted at last to have found a useful exercise in which to engage, the committee devoted the balance of the day to identifying preconditions to any merger that might someday be proposed. They tousled with earnings requirements, partner-associate ratios and quality-of-practice standards. By sunset, the committee had ferreted out only one precondition. But the members were unanimous in their belief that the criterion was basic and, if not met, would nip any merger possibility in the bud. They drafted a memo to the Executive Committee:

To: The Executive Committee
From: The Long-Range Planning Committee
Re: Adoption of Merger Precondition

At our most recent meeting, we adopted the following precondition to considering any merger:

The firm of Fairweather Winters & Sommers shall not merge with another firm unless the name of the surviving firm shall begin with Fairweather.

Malpractice for Fun and Profit

The FWS Insurance Committee convenes bi-monthly to review the firm's insurance needs and to moan about the bi-monthly increases in premiums. Occasionally, members of the committee are invited to speak on topics in which they have developed particular proficiency. At a recent meeting, the committee was privileged to hear a real veteran in the field of malpractice insurance, Manley A. Fairweather (no relation). Manley mustered his expertise in the school of hard knocks, having had the ill-fortune to be charged sixteen times with malpractice, sometimes unfairly. Here's what Manley had to say:

My friends, if there's a single word that will scare the bejeebers out of most lawyers, it's "malpractice." A group of words that will also generally do the trick is, "watch out for the bus," especially when shouted into the left ear of an attorney who is proofreading the final draft of an important brief.

Frequently, it is lack of sufficient attention that gives rise to malpractice. But not always. I would be among the first half dozen or so to concede that malpractice can crop up even when great attention is devoted to a matter.

Why, I remember one of the first malpractice cases ever brought against me. I had poured over a complaint day after day, polishing up a phrase here, correcting a spelling error there, slipping in a key comma or two and a pithy old English proverb that I was sure would knock the judge's eye out. Well, damned if that sneaky old statute of limitations didn't run out on me.

Historically, of course, malpractice was invented by lawyers to punish dumb doctors. Frequently, some idiot surgeon would leave a scalpel or credit card in a patient's abdomen. Often it would languish there undiscovered for years, sometimes long after the credit card had expired. In any case, this seemed to be carrying the notion of "don't leave home without it" to ridiculous extremes—and the courts so held.

But we lawyers have come to rue the day that we conceived of malpractice. Cruelly, it has been twisted against us. "Hoist with our own petard," the literati have said, confident that few, if any, of us would know what they were talking about.

Enough history, though.

To date, millions of dollars in grants have been expended to research the question of what causes legal malpractice. And yet, there is little persuasive evidence that malpractice is genetically linked. Nor is there much to suggest that the many anti-malpractice sprays and lotions that have flooded the market of late give more than a few hours of protection, even less if you are sweating profusely in the hot sun or decide at the last moment to go in for a cool, refreshing dip. The best of the lot, by all accounts, is Judi-tone, though those of you with fair skin may opt for Mal-Bloc without fear of ridicule or reprisal from this speaker.

But so what if malpractice has proven an enigma to geneticists and impervious to the best sprays and lotions thus far developed? Should we on that account toss in the terry and seek out a new profession? I say, "No!"

Should we instead seek legislation to bar or limit malpractice actions against lawyers? Not a bad idea; unconstitutional perhaps, but not a bad idea.

But we should first ask ourselves: "Is malpractice, in truth, as bad as people think? Or worse, maybe? Or not so bad? Is there a silver lining such as may be found in many clouds? And, if so, why?"

Certainly these questions deserve attention.

For those of you who see malpractice as an omnipresent demon ready to pounce on your head at every turn, it may help to put the problem in perspective. It may also help to see a psychiatrist, especially if you are covered by our firm's extended medical coverage, which provides a lifetime psychiatric benefit of $22,384.18 per family.

But let's take a concrete example. This will assist those of us who have some difficulty with abstractions to hone in on the issue. Suppose your client, let's call him Sid, comes into your office. First off, you offer Sid a cup of coffee, free. Sid explains that he has spoken to Frodo about the latter supplying all of Sid's needs for bathtubs with the new portable FrodoTubs® and that Frodo seems prepared to do so on certain terms which Sid explains to you. Sid tells you that he wants you to "make it legal." You obtain a chubby retainer from Sid and tell Sid "not to worry, Sid." You draft an airtight contract, have Sid sign it and put it in your file drawer without presenting it to Frodo for his signature.

Malpractice? Not so fast, Hernandez.

First of all, probably nobody will ever notice that the contract wasn't fully signed. So little of what we lawyers do bears any relationship to reality that chances are minuscule of any of our actions making any difference whatsoever, let alone becoming the subject of a malpractice claim. This thought should be a source of constant comfort to us.

But even in the unlikely event that the error surfaces, you will be in danger of a malpractice claim only if the error has an adverse impact on Sid. If my past experience is any guide, there is roughly a 62 percent chance that the error will prove a stroke of absolute genius. For example, Sid may find somebody who can supply portable bathtubs for half Frodo's price, or superior quality tubs for the same price. In either such case you would face not malpractice, but rather only embarrassingly laudatory praise.

And that's not the only thing that stands between you and malpractice. Even if Frodo refuses to deliver, Sid may be able to get the tubs from somebody else (no damages); you can claim that Sid was going to get the contract signed by Frodo (it wasn't your fault); if you're a big enough mogul in the bar association, Sid may not be able to find anybody willing to sue or to testify against you; Sid may not have been hurt badly enough to justify him suing, or may have been so ruined financially by your error that he can't afford to pay an attorney to sue you; or your defense lawyer may convince the jury, judge or appeals court that tucking contracts away half signed is standard operating procedure, and therefore not malpractice.

But, although the chances of your getting tagged with a malpractice judgment are relatively slim, malpractice strikes when you least expect it. And it hits old and rich, young and poor, black and white alike. So as my old constitutional law professor used to say, "Better safe than sorry."

And that's where the work of our committee becomes so important. If one of us gets socked with a malpractice judgment, the insurance company we hire pays off our poor client (excluding, of course, the attorneys' fees that the unlucky bastard has had to incur in order to collect). We then raise our hourly billing rates to cover the increased malpractice premium we'll have to pay to protect ourselves against our next error.

Editor's Note

At this point Manley was interrupted to take an important phone call. Sid was on the line and he was furious. He'd called Frodo to demand delivery of his FrodoTubs®, the retail price of which had quadrupled. They were the hottest items in town.

Frodo told Sid that his attorney advised him that he was free to sell to whomever he wanted. Frodo had chosen to sell to Sid's competitor, TubWorld.

Manley put Sid on hold and called Fred at Lawyers' Casualty, FWS's insurance carrier. "You're not going to believe what happened," said Manley. Fred believed—and checked his rate table to calculate FWS's new premium.

ADMINISTRATION

Introduction

A long with the need to treat our law firm as a business came the need to deal with all sorts of administrative details—keeping the office tidy, staying abreast of technology, assuring that we had adequate space to house our growing firm, keeping the troops happy and making sure that the firm did not run afoul of increasingly thorny ethical constraints, to name a few. To deal as inefficiently as possible with all of these issues, we created a plethora of additional committees.

All of this, I suppose, is the price of success. But looking back over the pieces in the section you are about to read, I wish we'd considered failure a more viable alternative.

Gripe No More

"Hiya!" "How're ya doin'?" "Great to see you!" "Just swell, and you?" "What's the good word, old buddy?" "You look terrific. Lose some weight?" "Everything's coming up roses."

From the chitchat, a person only moderately familiar with the art of committee identification at Fairweather, Winters & Sommers would know, in a trice, that he had happened in on a meeting of the FWS Committee on Associate Morale. Known around the firm as Grins and Mopes, the committee was born of Stanley J. Fairweather's conviction that a happy firm is a profitable firm. Conceived originally to deal with associate morale issues, the committee's jurisdiction had expanded to encompass everyone except partners.

Committee Chair Emanuel Candoo opened the meeting. "Okay, what's eating people around this place today?"

"Well, Manny, our most immediate problem seems to be the impending word-processing department strike, scheduled for three this afternoon," offered Lance Byte, Morale Committee liaison to word processing.

"What's the trouble? Higher wages, longer vacations, what?" demanded Harriet Akers.

"No. They seem altogether satisfied with those things," Lance reported. "They say they're bored. Everything seems repetitive. Nothing really new, they say."

"Well of course, their work is repetitive," said the Chair. "For Chrissakes, that's the whole idea of having a word-processing department. If they wanted to do something new, they should have become members of this committee. Every time I think I've heard it all, something like this comes along. A word-processing department that wants non-repetitive work. Can anybody suggest how to deal with this? Yes, Harriet."

"Well, maybe they could rotate the projects so that each time a project comes back for revision it would go to a different person in the department. Then the work wouldn't seem so repetitive to them."

"Excellent idea, Harriet. Lance, why don't you take that one back to the word processors and see how it flies? Now, what other problems do we have? David?"

"Duplication is unhappy. They've got too many rush orders. They want a new rule that only requires them to return a job within 48 hours of when it's brought to them. They say that, unless this demand is met, they will begin omitting pages at random from the documents they copy."

"Why, that's sabotage, or blackmail, or maybe both!

They can't do that. I'll have them all canned!" shouted Chair Candoo.

"Now, Manny, relax; you can't fire them," David Alms assured him. "For one thing, it would be an unfair labor practice under the agreement you signed with their union last year. For another thing, if you did can them, they would code those little boxes that give us access to the machines so that it would be years before we ever made a copy again. I think that, like good lawyers, we should know when the other side has the cards and bargain for the best deal we can get. I'll bet that, if we're real nice to them, we can get them to cut the turnaround time to 40 hours."

"Okay, do it then. Bargain with them. Who's next?" asked Emanuel.

"I guess I am," said Otto Flack, "and I'm sorry to report that the paralegals are not at all pleased."

"What is it this time? Last month we got them business cards, and the month before, we got them their own offices and secretaries."

"They just don't feel that they're being treated properly. After all, they *are* paraprofessionals. For example, they were not invited to the last three semi-weekly attorney dinner-dances we implemented a week and a half ago in response to associate criticism of a slack social schedule. They've banded together and say that, unless a list of thirty-seven demands is met, they will not abstract any more depositions or answer a single interrogatory. Unfortunately, I think they're serious."

"What the hell, let's invite them to the dinner-dances. They certainly can't make them any duller. And if it will make them happy, why, that's what we're in business for."

"Man, I hate to add to our problems, but we find ourselves with a very glum messenger corps," reported messenger liaison Patrick Conshenz.

"We just got them a new waiting room with lounge chairs, sofas, fully stocked bar, and a color TV. So it can't be their working conditions. Don't tell me they're demanding secretarial help."

"No. Actually, they're concerned that they often have to do their messengering in inclement weather. While neither rain nor sleet nor snow may stop the United States Mail, our messengers feel free to adhere to a slightly less rigorous standard. The complaints were prompted by the fact that, within the last several months, three messengers have contracted rather severe drippy noses."

"What are they demanding?"

"Really, they are being quite reasonable. They have given us three options. The first is for the messengers not to have to deliver messages in weather that, by majority vote of the messengers, is determined to be nasty. The second is for the firm to outfit them with new mackintoshes and hats, down coats with hoods, gloves, and appropriate footwear. The third is for the firm to hire limos with drivers to cart them around when they run errands in nasty weather. Myself, I favor the second option. It would give them a more uniform look and thus enhance the image of the office."

"Do we have to give them our answer today, or may we take it under advisement?"

"They've placed no deadlines on us, so we can take our time. Of course, until we decide, there will be no deliveries or pickups in nasty weather."

"Lawrence, I see you have your hand up. Would the secretaries like to bring something to the attention of the Morale Committee?"

"Well since you mentioned it, there is just one thing, Manny. They've asked me to convey to you their desire to be considered for across-the-board 32 percent salary increases and, further, their request that a pool equal to 7.2 percent of the gross income of the firm be set aside for bonuses to them. They think this is only fair."

"Frankly, though of course I wouldn't want this to get back to them, it strikes me as a bit excessive."

By this time, the committee had become glum. There

seemed little hope that all of the demands that had been presented to the members at the meeting could be met. And if they could not all be met, then there would be groups at FWS who were not happy. And when there were groups at FWS who were not happy, then the members of the Morale Committee, whose job it was to keep everybody happy, were themselves unhappy. And since Stanley Fairweather had said that it was a happy firm that was a profitable one, it stood to reason that an unhappy firm would be an unprofitable one. And that would make Stanley unhappy. And when Stanley was unhappy, nobody, but nobody, was happy.

Thinking it best that he take his licks now, the Chair asked his secretary to see if Stanley could join the meeting for a minute. When Stanley came in, Manny explained the demands that had been made on the committee. Stanley thought for a moment and spoke.

"Some time ago I sensed that people had a few things they were unhappy about and no place to bring their unhappinesses," said Stanley. "I thought that if people had complaints and no way to resolve them, they would be unhappy. And a happy firm, I always thought, was a profitable one.

"So I set up this committee. And, for a while, it worked pretty well. Somewhere along the way, though, things got all mixed up. People got the idea that, because there was a place to bring their complaints, they had to have complaints to bring. And as each complaint was handled, people thought that their next complaint had to be even bigger. And they became unhappy unless each complaint was resolved the way they wanted it resolved.

"So, instead of resolving morale problems, the Morale Committee has begun to create them and aggravate them. And, of course, resolving complaints takes money, which makes the firm less profitable. So the Morale Committee has lately made the firm neither happy nor profitable.

"As of today, then, I am abolishing this committee. I still think a happy firm is a profitable one, but there may be better ways to register our complaints than by bringing them to a committee. Tomorrow I will have a punching bag installed in the coffee room."

And as they walked out of the conference room, the former members of the Morale Committee agreed among themselves that they felt a lot happier already.

A Tidy Mess

Lt. Colonel Clinton Hargraves, retired, U.S. Army; certified public accountant; and Fairweather, Winters & Sommers Firm Administrator, was distraught. And House Committee Chairman, Seymour Plain, knew exactly why. Only last week, the Colonel had circulated one of his famous memos:

```
To: All Personnel — Legal, Non-legal and
       Paralegal
From: Lt. Colonel Clinton Hargraves, CPA
Subject: Filth
```

This fine Firm can be proud of many things. We have fine lawyers and an equally fine support staff. Our work is top-flight, our reputation unsullied. We have struggled to meet many enemies, and they are ours. Only one victory seems to have eluded our fine Firm: victory over grime. As I stride daily through our fine offices, it pains me to see messy desks, files strewn about, coats flung over file cabinets, boxes in the halls. It is not a pretty sight. We are not a Firm of slobs. I have been privileged to see the insides of many of your homes and they are, almost without exception, ship-shape. The Firm needs to make its work-home as beautiful as our home-homes. The Firm needs all of your cooperation in this beautification endeavor. Let us all pitch in to make the Firm's offices both spic and span.

But, on his rounds of the office today, the Colonel found the same mess he'd been encountering for months. Worse, he found copies of his Filth Memo strewn about. This caused him to seek the counsel of the House Committee, under whose jurisdiction filth fell.

"Seymour, I'm at a loss. I thought my last memo would really turn things around," said the Colonel.

"It did have some real grabbers," said Rachel Steinberg. "I especially liked the concept of work-home and home-home."

"Thanks, Rachel."

"And I thought it was great that you spoke of 'victory over grime.' That was very inspiring," added Heather Regale.

"But, fact is, it hasn't worked, right?" T. Wm. Williams (known, affectionately, as T-Bills) summoned the group back to earth.

"Right. I think we may need a whole new approach," suggested Gary Swath.

"That just might work," said the Colonel.

"What?" asked Chairman Plain, confused.

"A whole new approach. Now how about this. What if we bring all of this down to the bottom line, what filth costs. I have figures on what we spend on clean-up on a monthly basis. We could add in several hours per secretary per week, multiply that out, calculate the number of files we generate in a month, and divide that into total costs to get a gross filth cost per file. If we were cleaner, we could probably condense the number of files we used, so we should figure in a supply savings factor and, of course, the reduced space use in the file room. From there, we add in the actuarial . . ."

"Hang on there, Colonel, you just lost your audience," advised Heather. "I don't think this is one we sell on economics."

"Heather's right, Colonel," T-Bills agreed. "We need more than that."

"How about some sort of inspection?" asked the Colonel. "I'd walk around, say two to five times a day, unannounced. Anything's out of order—zap, we dock 'em a day's pay. I'd have those suckers in line in no time. Why, in 'Nam we'd go into the barracks and . . ."

"Colonel, that won't fly," said Rachel. "Though you may regard office filth as a war, that's not the majority view."

"Maybe we need a more positive approach," suggested Heather. "Instead of docking people's pay, we could reward them for good performance. What if you were to walk around, say once a week, and award a prize for the cleanest area of the firm? We could announce it in the office bulletin, have a little plaque in the coffee room."

"Great idea," said the Colonel.

"No, I think we'd just get a lot of flack. People wouldn't take it seriously, I'm afraid," said the Chair.

"You're probably right," said the Colonel. "Maybe if I circulated another memo, worded a bit stronger."

"No, I doubt if that would do it, Colonel. Maybe we should just hire more clean-up staff to do the work," Gary suggested.

"Trouble with that is that we'd have a constant wave of people swarming through the office with garbage bags. I don't think that would enhance the atmosphere much," said the Colonel.

"We could try getting used to a little filth," offered T-Bills. "You oughta see my kids' rooms. After awhile, it's not so bad."

"That's not funny," said Rachel.

"What we really need," mused Chairman Plain, "is something that would give this campaign some respectability, some credibility."

"Stanley," both Heather and Gary said, in unison.

As if on cue, Stanley J. Fairweather entered the room. "Hi there, Committee. Oh, hello, Colonel, what're *you* doing here? Listen, I just stopped by to say that we've got to do something about the way this office looks. It's a sty."

"Just what we were talking about, Stanley. Do you have any ideas?" asked the Chair.

"Well, Seymour, I was thinking that maybe a memo coming from me, trying to instill a little pride, might just do the trick. Why don't you folks give me a week or so to try something out?"

The House Committee, stymied itself, was only too happy to turn the problem over to Stanley. And within a week, the cleanliness of the office took a dramatic turn for the better. Though the Colonel thought it just might be a delayed reaction to his Filth Memo, others attributed it to a simple memo from Stanley Fairweather.

My Friends:

It's time we tidied up a bit. I'd sure appreciate it if you'd help. And, remember—Cleanliness is next to Stanleyness.

Stanley J. Fairweather

Just the Fax, Please, Ma'am

The Fairweather Winters & Sommers Committee Overseeing Management of Modern Innovative Technology Tending to Ensure Efficiency, known as the COMMITTEE Committee, was awaiting the arrival of its Chair, Robert Mentor.

"Where the hell is Rob?" wondered committee member Ruth Tender.

"Meeting was s'posed to start twenty minutes ago."

"Why don't we call him?" suggested Lydia Dos.

"Good idea, Ms. Dos," offered the firm administrator, Lt. Colonel (retired) Clinton Hargraves, CPA. "I'll do it. How do you work this damn phone?"

"You have to pick up the receiver, the thing that's shaped a little like a banana," said Arthur Fortran.

"Very funny, Art. I mean the speaker phone."

"Just push that little black switch and hold it down for a second, Colonel," said Lydia.

"Thanks. Hey, it's easy."

"Hello," the Chair answered.

" 'lo, Rob, you coming?"

"Who is that, coming where?" asked Rob.

"Colonel."

"You in a cave, for godsake, Clint?"

"No, I'm on the speaker phone."

"Well get off of that damn thing, would ya?"

"Okay, just a sec. Damn, cut him off."

Within minutes, Mentor appeared in the conference room. "Sorry, forgot about the meeting. I put it into my daily diary on the computer, but I keep forgetting to look at my computer."

"Why don't you just print the diary out?" suggested Arthur.

"Can't," said Robert. "I don't have a printer, so I have to go through word processing to print it out, and they're always so backed up that by the time I print out today's diary, it's tomorrow."

"Well, maybe we should just get more printers put in," said Arthur.

"Nope, the Finance Committee would never approve that; it costs a fortune. And besides, we're not wired for it," said Robert.

"Not wired for it, what do you mean?" asked Arthur.

"We don't have the voltage or ampage or some damnage. If we were to put in printers, the lights on the east side of the office would fade in and out, unless we restricted use of the printers to between midnight and 6 A.M."

"Well, that's not very good," said Lydia. "Can't we rewire?"

"No, we're moving to a new building in two-and-a-half years, and the Executive Committee wants to avoid capital expenditures until then," said the Colonel.

"Rob, doesn't that kill the other things on the agenda we were going to talk about?" asked Ruth.

"No. If we decide to install the voice mail or buy more FAX machines, we can take them with us to the new building."

"Voice mail? What's voice mail?" asked the Colonel.

"That's so when you're out, somebody can leave a message for you," explained Lydia.

"Big deal. They can do that now, with my secretary," said Arthur.

"Yes, but what if your secretary is away?"

"Then it goes to the receptionist," said Arthur.

"With voice mail, you can leave a personalized message on the machine for people who call you," explained Ruth.

"A personalized message, why would I do that?"

"Let's suppose you're expecting a call from your client Sam Smith, for whom you're litigating an important matter. The other side has just made a settlement offer of $25 million, which will expire at the end of the day. You've got to go out to an important meeting, but you leave a message for Sam that they've offered to settle for 25 mil and you recommend he accept it, and would he please leave you a message by 5 P.M. Understand?"

"That's preposterous."

"Preposterous?"

"Yes. First, I don't have any client named Sam Smith. Second, I do estate planning, not litigation. And third, if I did litigate and anyone offered me $25 million, I'd grab it and worry about old Sam Smith later."

"She was just giving you a hypothetical," Lydia protested.

"Well try to make your hypotheticals a bit more realistic. But I wouldn't leave a message like that, anyway. What if somebody else called and got the message? What about the attorney-client privilege?"

"You give Sam a special code that he has to punch in in order to get the message, so that if somebody doesn't have the code, they can't get Sam's message."

"You mean you have to record a separate message for everyone who might call and leave it in a special place and give them a code number, which they have to remember, and then I have to change the message every time I want to leave a new one?" asked the Colonel.

"It's really not nearly as complicated as it seems, Colonel."

"Not complicated? You're talking to a guy who can't operate a speaker phone."

"Maybe we should defer action on the voice mail proposal and get the representative of Tell-It-Like-It-Is Software to come back to demonstrate how it works for the Colonel and for anyone else who wants to watch it."

"Good idea," said Robert. "Maybe we can take care of the last item, though, these additional FAX machines. Anyone object to our getting three more of them?"

"How do those damn FAX things work, anyway?" asked the Colonel.

"What difference does it make?" asked Mentor.

"Well, I figure we're a committee on technology, we ought to know something about how things work," said the Colonel. "And those FAX machines seem like magic to me."

"Actually, they're very simple, Clint," said Lydia. "Each machine has a tiny guy inside, lying on his back. As the sheet comes through, the guy calls his buddy in the other machine and reads it to him and that guy types it onto a sheet that's coming out of his machine."

"You're a riot, Lydia. But I don't understand why we need more machines. We just bought two a few months ago," Ruth complained.

"Our usage is way up. All of our clients have them, and other law firms seem to use them more often than they use the U.S. Mail," said Mentor.

"But those machines cost over a thousand bucks each," said Arthur; "we can't be running out and buying more every month."

"Nonsense, we can't afford *not* to," said Lydia. "The Colonel here came up with the idea of billing for both incoming and outgoing FAXes at a buck a page. And now, next to photocopying, FAXing is the most profitable thing our firm does. If we were smart, we'd give up practicing law altogether and just go into the photocopy/FAX business—Fairweather, Photocopy & FAX."

"But I like to practice law," protested Arthur.

"Don't worry, Art," Robert reassured him, "we'd continue practicing law—as a loss leader."

Outer Space

With the firm fairly bursting its britches from recent hiring and client snatching coups, the FWS Space Committee, whose members are known affectionately (behind their backs) as the Space Cadets, met Thursday last in emergency closed-door session in the firm supply room. Chair T. Wm. Williams articulated the question before them succinctly as being "basically one of what to do." Embellishing slightly, he reminded the committee that neither nook nor cranny was available in which to stash the forty new associate and summer student bodies that the Hiring Committee had bagged. In his view, the choices boiled down to fewer than three—to wit, taking additional space to house a segment of the firm or packing up the entire firm and moving it en masse to a new location.

Penelope Pincher interrupted to suggest that, before rushing to take on more space, we should explore whether there might be ways to utilize our existing space more effectively so as to obviate, or at least forestall, the need for a move. Penny confessed that, in violation of committee rules, she'd afforded the matter some advance thought and had developed suggestions ranging from compressing the space squandered on associates by tossing them all into the library for their first half decade or so with the firm, to eliminating the space consumed by senior partners by enforcing the mandatory retirement age, to increasing the numbers of offices by rebuilding to make all of them (except Stanley Fairweather's) one-third smaller.

These suggestions were discarded for different reasons, the first because of the devastating effect it might have on hiring, the second because nobody had the guts to do it, and the third because of a widespread suspicion that it was a crummy idea. Ms. Pincher was chastised for wasting committee time, the Chair noting that this confirmed the genius of the committee rule that proscribed advance thought.

Greater efficiency seeming thus improbable, discussion turned to whether the entire firm should move, or whether additional space should be sought for only a portion of the firm.

Through a flip of the coin, the committee reasoned that it should consider first the possibility of taking additional space. Since no contiguous space was available in the building, the choice was between noncontiguous space in the building or space in a building across the street.

Ms. Pincher pointed out that remaining totally within the same building would have the decided advantage of allowing the firm to utilize fully the stock of stationery that the Supplies Committee Subcommittee on Stationery had ordered.

Godfrey Bleschieu added his strong preference for taking additional space in the same building. Otherwise, he feared, in inclement weather firm members would run across the street to the satellite office without their coats on, and wind up sick as dogs or more so.

Apologizing for being money grubbing, Dolly Fu Lish pointed out that rental in the building across the street was $18 per square foot less dear than space in the current building. Since, recent history notwithstanding, the firm was designed to be a for-profit venture, the rental differential, she argued, was not patently irrelevant.

Reserving, for the nonce, judgment on the question of whether to move the whole damn firm or only a portion thereof, the committee pondered who, if only a portion of the firm moved, would move. The alternatives, and the rationales thereof, being obvious to all, were, therefore, expounded upon at considerable length. It will here suffice to enumerate them briefly.

Transporting an entire department of the firm's practice, some thought, would preserve the camaraderie of persons working in the same area. Others, questioning whether camaraderie existed to preserve, nonetheless supported the proposition enthusiastically as a good way to get the dolts in the real estate department the hell out of the office.

Shifting a cross-section of the firm's practice, on the other hand, would permit lawyers in one department ready access to the counsel of lawyers in the other areas of the practice. And even if this counsel were not sought, it might promote greater interaction among lawyers, which was thought desirable by one-quarter of those in attendance.

Another alternative was to jettison a segment of the firm's non-legal staff, such as bookkeeping or word processing, thus keeping all the lawyers together. But severe doubts about whether these other departments could be trusted to work if they were off on their own truncated the popularity of this suggestion. Furthermore, such a move would be untenable, since it would afford some of the non-legal staff better views of Lake Michigan than some lawyers who remained in the present office would have.

Finally, there were those who thought that the non-contiguous space should be used as a sort of penalty box to which those in disfavor with the higher-ups could be banished.

For most, the issue of whom to isolate paled by comparison to the central question of whether the carpeting in the non-contiguous space would be the same as in the current office. Several felt strongly that having the same carpeting in the new space would make the non-contiguous space seem "more contiguous," but worried whether the identical dye lot would be available eighteen years later. Others thought that something new, perhaps in a thick beige pile, would hit the spot. But Chairman Williams insisted on sweeping this issue under the rug.

Dolly, who was particularly wont to wonder aloud, wondered aloud whether this might not be a propitious time to establish a branch office in another city, thus solving the space problem by shipping a significant number of lawyers clean out of the city.

Lacking consensus on whom to move if non-contiguous space were rented, the committee shifted to a discussion of where the entire firm might be plopped.

Harvey Holdem suggested that an orderly approach to the matter would be to identify all of the buildings with sufficient space to house the firm and to consider seriatim whether any was acceptable.

While not disputing that that would be an orderly approach, Harry Ratchet moved that the firm rent four floors in Flashy Towers. In support of the motion, he pointed out that Flashy was being developed by a new firm client, and taking space there would help solidify our grasp on the client.

In opposition, Laurence Highner argued that we knew that our client tended to skimp on quality. But the movant pounced on this remark as unethical, claiming that it was learned in the course of a confidential attorney-client relationship and was, therefore, privileged.

Fighting ethical fire with fire, Highner continued to object by asking rhetorically how then we could negotiate our lease, since we had drafted the form.

"Quite well," replied Ratchet.

But as the committee delved more into both the nitty and the gritty, it became clear that Flashy had fatal flaws. For one thing, another law firm had already rented space on a higher floor than would be available to FWS. And even more importantly, the building was a full six blocks from the Chicago Northwestern suburban commuter train station.

Just as Highner began to extol the advantages of the firm constructing its own building, Harry Punctillio, Executive Committee member, burst in exclaiming that he had been looking all over for the Space Committee. He had, he said, some good news and some bad news. A majority of the committee having opted to hear the good news first, Harry announced that the firm space problem had been solved, at least temporarily. The bad news was that the solution had come about because the entire labor law department had seceded from the firm.

A Firm, By Any Other Name

Not since Fairbut Cooler's death, some twenty years ago, had the Fairweather firm been faced with the prospect of a name change. Many at the firm had become convinced that having one's name in the firm name brought not only prosperity, but immortality as well. Although neither Mr. Fairweather, Mr. Winters nor Mr. Sommers was *in extremis*, the Executive Committee, in its wisdom, entrusted to the Long-Range Planning Committee the question of what ought to happen in the unlikely event that one of these supposedly semi-retired senior partners should chance to become reacquainted with his Maker.

"It seems to me that the answer is simple: we just drop the name of whoever dies and add the next name on the list," suggested Rudolph Grossbladt. Having long dreamed of the day his name would adorn the reception area, Grossbladt now found himself a scant two deaths away from that goal. "That's what we've always done in the past," he added.

"Just because we've always done it in the past doesn't necessarily mean we're going to do it in the future, you know," said Sylvia Wurrier.

"But it usually does," replied Rudy.

"Well, I still think we ought to consider other alternatives," suggested Hiram Miltoast.

"Such as?" challenged Rudy.

"Such as leaving the firm name the way it is. I think Fairweather, Winters & Sommers has a nice ring to it. And since it's been intact for over twenty years, it's recognized in the profession. I think it would be a shame to give that up."

"Besides," Penelope Pincher agreed, "it costs money to change the stationery, we'd have to send announcements and we'd have to change the silver lettering on the wall in the reception area. Not only that, but we'd have to get new business cards for everyone. With the price of silver, stationery and cards, you're not talking peanuts."

"Well, I don't think we should let a few dollars stand in the way of an important decision like this," argued Rudy.

"Well, if we just drop the name of the partner who died, the additional cost wouldn't be that great," Penelope continued; "we wouldn't have to get any new silver letters for the reception area. And as far as the stationery goes, we could even leave it as is for awhile, until we run out, or we could just X out the name of the deceased. That would be in keeping with the trend toward shorter firm names, anyway."

"Just dropping the name of the deceased partner is not so easy, either," Rudy reminded the committee; "the surviving spouse doesn't take kindly to it. Remember how Evelyn Cooler begged us to keep Fairbut's name up there?"

"Evelyn? Was that her name? I didn't even remember."

"You probably remember her nickname. She was such a frail little thing, people called her Slightly."

"Oh yes, Slightly Cooler, now I remember."

"Maybe to avoid problems with the surviving spouse, we should retain all of the present names until each of the named partners passes on and then drop them all, just call the firm '&' or maybe '&, P.C.' "

"That's not funny, Rudolph," Sylvia opined.

"Who's joking? I think that's what our partnership agreement provides."

"Nobody looks at that, anyway."

"Wait a minute. I think we're not analyzing this as

lawyers," Miltoast objected. "We're assuming that the answer to our question of what happens to the firm name is the same no matter who dies. I think we ought to take them one at a time. Let's first assume that Stanley dies, then we take Oscar and finally we'll take James."

"Now wait a minute. This is getting a little bit too ghoulish for me," said Rudy. "I'm not going to sit around here and speculate on which of my partners is going to die next."

"Or whether any of them is ever going to die," added James Freeport.

"Yes, next thing you know, there'll be a pool," offered Rudy.

"I got five says it's Oscar," Hiram pulled his billfold from his back pocket; "he's been wheezing like crazy lately."

"Hey, you stop that!" shouted Sylvia.

"Sorry, only kidding."

"Look, I think maybe we've identified most of the possible alternatives, and none of them seems to be very satisfactory. Maybe we should run a 'name the firm' contest. We'd throw it open to all clients and staff at the firm; lawyers and their immediate families would be ineligible. We could come up with a nice prize for the winner," Penny offered.

"Naw, I think that sounds a little too hokey, maybe even unprofessional," Sylvia replied.

Frustrated that none of his arguments had carried the day, Rudy Grossbladt abandoned the facade of sound firm policy in favor of a personal plea of fairness. "We've got a bunch of people here who have relied on the firm practice of removing the name of a partner who dies and adding the name of the next in line. Several of us never would have stayed around here if we'd have known you were going to change the rules in the middle of the game.

"As young associates we aspired to partnership, as young partners we aspired to a corner office, as corner partners we aspired to a place on the Executive Committee, and as Executive Committee members all that we have left to aspire to is a place in the firm name. And now some of you are going to take even that away from us.

"How do you think it made me feel when my daughter graduated from law school last year and went out and formed her own firm with a friend? At the opening of her office, they had a little open house. They served wine and cheese. A '79 Chenin Blanc, if I recall correctly—lacked body—and the brie was too soft. But anyway, I walked into that reception and there it was in silver letters— Grossbladt—her name, my name, up there in silver. I'd worked all of my life to achieve that and she had it right out of law school."

"Well, Rudy, we ought to consider what it means to be changing the firm name constantly. I think that the firm has become an institution by now, and that it's not appropriate for us to be changing our name all the time," argued Miltoast. "You don't see General Motors changing their name, do you?"

"Maybe we should go to something more like 'General Motors' then," James suggested. "How about 'The Law Firm' ? It's got a nice, solid, generic sound to it."

"No, we're not ready to go to anything like that, not yet anyway."

"But I think Hiram is right. We have become an institution, an institution under the name of Fairweather, Winters & Sommers, and I think we ought to stick with that name."

Lacking a better solution, after only another six hours of discussion, the Long-Range Planning Committee resolved "to make the firm name 'Fairweather, Winters & Sommers' forever, or until such time as the Executive Committee shall change its mind." Only Rudolph Grossbladt dissented.

Postscript

Although committee members had known that Grossbladt's views were strongly held, they had no idea how strongly until a month later, when they received an invitation to an open house. There Rudy Grossbladt proudly poured the vintage champagne, sliced the firm brie and pointed exuberantly to the silver letters that spelled out "Grossbladt, Grossbladt & Jenkins," explaining that his daughter had consented graciously to his name being the first Grossbladt.

Rudy lived on happily for many years at Grossbladt, Grossbladt & Jenkins, having learned at last what every good lawyer must—when you think you've come to the end of the line, there's always another alternative. And when he died, in the fullness of his time, Rudy's daughter would leave his name right where it was.

Ethics In the Air

"I'm not sure it's an ethical problem," said Patrick Conshenz.

"Of course it's an ethical problem," opined Ethics Committee Chair Lydia Milife.

"How can we tell for sure? I mean, I wouldn't want to get into something outside the scope of our jurisdiction," said Patrick, worried. "That would be unethical."

"We could go to the Committee on Committees for a jurisdictional ruling," suggested Ellen Jane Ritton.

"No, that would delay us for at least a year," moaned Lydia.

"Well, I say we bite the bullet," suggested Stephan Mestrow.

"Let's deliberate. In fact, I move that we deliberate."

"Second," said Ellen Jane.

"We don't need a motion to deliberate," said Lydia; "just do it."

"Without a motion, are you sure, Lydia?" asked Stephan.

"Absolutely, and I so rule."

"Okay, then with the permission of my second, I withdraw my motion to deliberate," said Stephan.

"Permission granted," Ellen Jane said, emphatically.

"Good, now we can get to the heart of the matter— what do we do about frequent flier miles?" said the Chair.

"I say that whoever flies 'em, keeps 'em," offered Gerald Forspiel; "sort of finders keepers, losers weepers, if you know what I mean."

" 'Finders keepers' hardly seems to be an appropriate ethical principle," protested Ellen Jane.

"Maybe not," said Stephan, "but it does resolve the issue neatly. And there's something to be said for that."

"But why should the person who just happens to be called upon for a trip be entitled to personal use of the miles he or she accumulates?" asked Patrick.

"How about because they have to walk through that damn mile-long United neon corridor at O'Hare? Besides, who's more entitled?" asked Stephan.

"What about the client on whose behalf the lawyer flew? That client paid for the flight; why shouldn't it be entitled to the benefit of the frequent flier miles?" asked Ellen Jane.

"Well, I suppose, then, that if I fly for a client and don't eat the little foil pouch of roasted peanuts, I'll have to send that to the client, too. After all, fair is fair; the client paid," said Lydia.

"And the plastic gizmo that you stir the drink with, and the inflight magazine," added Stephan.

"You're carrying this too far, and you both know it," Ellen Jane protested. "I think that we can distinguish between something of obvious value, such as frequent flier miles, and a pouch of nuts."

"Well, what would you suggest we do when we make a trip on behalf of more than one client?" asked Stephan.

"Why, I suppose you simply split up the mileage between the clients," answered Patrick.

"Equally, or in proportion to the number of hours billed to each client?" asked Lydia.

"That reminds me of an ethical question that's always troubled me," said Forspiel. "Let's say you're flying from New York to Los Angeles for one client and, on the plane, you work for another client for two hours of the six-hour flight. Do you bill the client you're flying for six hours and the other two? or four and two? or what?"

"Well, obviously, you can't bill six and two because that would be billing eight hours for six elapsed hours," said Patrick. "That would be unethical."

"Aha! But would it? What if, for example, you were flying from Los Angeles to New York instead? Because of the time difference, nine hours would have elapsed. Does that mean you can bill nine hours west-to-east, but only six (or, come to think of it, three) east-to-west? Does that make sense? And what if it's daylight savings time, huh?"

"Ethics doesn't always make sense," cautioned Ellen Jane.

"Gerald, you raise some very difficult ethical issues, but I'd like to stick to the topic of frequent flier miles," said the Chair.

"We might be able to credit some of our clients for frequent flier miles and use them on other flights we take for those clients. But for many of our clients, we fly only infrequently. By the time we got around to generating enough mileage for an award, the miles may have elapsed," said Stephan. "Besides, and worse, do you realize the kind of bookkeeping headaches we'd create trying to keep accurate tabs on all of these miles?"

"Well, I doubt that we could eliminate an ethical problem on the grounds that it may create a little bookkeeping difficulty for us. Couldn't we simply allocate the bookkeeping charges to clients?" asked Ellen Jane.

"They'd exceed the value of the frequent flier miles," Lydia observed.

"Well, maybe we could solve this by getting our clients to waive any claim to frequent flier miles on flights we take for them," suggested Patrick. "I could prepare a draft Frequent Flier Waiver Form."

"Great idea. And if they won't waive? Or, what if some do, and some don't? Where are we then?" asked Stephan.

"We could require that all frequent flier miles be turned in to the firm and be used for travel on internal firm business," offered Ellen Jane. "That way, at least the full firm would benefit."

"How does that resolve the ethical question?" asked Patrick. "We still would be using benefits paid by clients for our own use."

"I've got an idea," said Stephan. "This problem arises only if we accumulate frequent flier miles, right?"

"Of course," said Patrick, "that's what we've been talking about for the last hour."

"So, no frequent flier miles, no ethical problem, right?"

"Right."

"So, all we have to do is prohibit our attorneys from putting in their frequent flier numbers when they fly on business."

"That just creates a windfall for the airlines," argued Ellen Jane.

"Ethics doesn't always make sense," echoed Stephan.

Lacking a better solution, the Ethics Committee voted unanimously to recommend to the Executive Committee that attorneys be prohibited from using frequent flier numbers when flying for clients. The Executive Committee elected to refer the matter to the Bar Association Ethics Committee, which, at this writing, is still wrestling with the problem.

Treated Like Dirt

In the brave new world of competition for legal business, some departments have fared far better than others. At FWS, Real Estate is one of the others.

Snap. The meeting of the Fairweather, Winters & Sommers Real Estate Department began. Meetings of that department always begin with a snap, the breaking of the twig that gives Phillip D. W. Wilson, III the necessary seisin to chair the meeting. Many unkind, but honest, lawyers say that the snap of the twig is the only snap that these meetings ever contain.

Manley "Jaguar" Fairweather (no relation), so called by his real estate colleagues because of his cat-like moves when faced with a potential springing use, opened the meeting by issuing the following complaint: when he had requested help from the Assignment Committee, he had been told that there were no associates available to work with him; all of them were tied up on litigation projects.

"We don't get no respect no more. When this firm came into prominence, it was us, the real estate department, that was its flagship. Why, we had some of the best charitable remaindermen in the business and, before women's lib, we had one of the best fee tail male clauses in the city, right in our office form warranty deed, thanks to the draftsmanship of Oscar Winters. And now we've sunken to the point where we can't even scare up a first-year associate for help on an important mortgage closing.

"I can understand how that could happen occasionally," Jag continued, "but it has now been eight-and-a-half months since I've been able to get any assistance from the Assignment Committee. And if I don't get some help pretty soon, that emergency mortgage loan that I requested the help on is going to close. I'm starting to get desperate."

Several members of the department expressed their sympathy with Jag, but none seemed surprised at the treatment that he had received, for two basic reasons. First, many other members had experienced similar treatment themselves and, second, Jag had complained about his treatment on this mortgage loan at each meeting for eight-and-a-half months now.

The Chair announced that one of the members of the department, Hiram Miltoast, had been honored by being selected to give the keynote address at the semiannual meeting of the Subcommittee on Zoning Variations of the Zoning Committee of the local bar association. "I hardly have to tell you what that means. Those luncheons frequently attract upwards of eleven people, and the speaker gets his lunch free and receives a certificate of appreciation suitable for framing. I know that you all share my pride in having one of our brothers selected for this honor."

At this point, the meeting broke into applause, and cries of "speech, speech" and "pass the thousand island dressing, dammit" fairly pierced the air. Responding to his public, Hiram rose to say a few words, first passing the dressing, which happened to have landed in front of him.

"Thank you very much, ladies and gentlemen," said Hiram. "You are very kind. Of course, I am flattered at having been chosen, but I certainly cannot take all of the credit. If it were not for the encouragement of Oscar and many of you here in this room, I might have given up my zoning variance work long ago. In my time of struggles, you stood behind me. Finally, I would be remiss if I failed to mention the role that our partner, Herb Gander, chair and sole member of the Speaker Selection Task Force of the Subcommittee on Zoning Variations, had in my receiving this honor."

Gander rose and protested that he had made the speaker selection solely on the basis of merit and that he resented the insinuation that he would use his position of power to reward some crony of his. Hiram said that he resented being called a crony, and especially a crony of somebody with Herb's reputation. Several members of the department assured Herb that Hiram had not intended to impugn his integrity, but merely to express his gratitude. Other members assured Hiram that Herb had not meant what he said literally either. Eventually, order was restored.

Jag suggested that Hiram's selection as speaker ought to be made known by the department to the rest of the firm, since it was further evidence of the esteem in which the real estate department is held by the local bar. "Some day, Allah and Stanley Fairweather willing, our own firm may recognize what an outstanding real estate department we are," said Jag. And several of the department members mumbled under their breath, "Amen."

The Chair next threw the meeting open for discussion of any unusual problems that had been encountered in the department in the last month. Percifal Snikkety said that he had had something of an unusual situation come up. "I was over at the title company checking the title to a piece of land that a client of mine was acquiring and reading the description in the tract book against the legal description contained in the deed, when I noticed sitting next to me a college-age kid, a little scruffy looking, carrying a 'No Nukes' sign. Well, I didn't think too much of it. It was a little unusual, of course, but it didn't seem to me to be any of my business. Anyway, I got up, just for a minute, to get another tract book and, when I came back, the No Nukes kid wasn't there any more. So I finished my business and went off to this closing. Just as I was about to hand over the check to the seller, I looked down at the deed and there, in big red letters across the top and bottom of the deed, was written 'NO NUKES.'

"Now, I thought to myself, this is a case of first impression so far as I know. Is a deed that has 'NO NUKES' written across it, in two places yet, but is otherwise valid, a valid deed? This question could not have arisen at common law. 'NO TRUNCHEONS,' perhaps. But not 'NO NUKES.' So I was faced with something of a choice. Do I put off the closing a day and perhaps blow the whole deal, do I phone the firm and have somebody run a Lexis search of 'NO NUKES' on quit claim deeds, or do I just wing it?"

Hiram could stand the suspense no longer, "Well, what did you do, huh, what did you do?" he asked.

"Well, I knew that it wouldn't make any sense to call the firm to get a Lexis search, because I never would get help from the Assignment Committee. And winging it isn't in the nature of a real estate lawyer. But I didn't want to blow the deal either, so I had to think quick. I called the other lawyer aside and we negotiated an indemnity in the event that the title conveyed to my client was adversely affected by the 'NO NUKES' on the deed. And I've placed a copy of the indemnity in the firm form file under 'Quit claim deed, no nuke indemnity.' "

"Good thinking, Percy," said Herb. "A lot of lawyers just don't realize how quick real estate lawyers have to be on their feet. It looks as if you saved the day for one of our clients again."

"Shucks, Herb, it weren't nothin'. All in a day's work—in the FWS real estate department."

Phillip reminded the group that they had to vacate the conference room soon because there was a meeting of the firm's lawyer league football squad scheduled to review last week's game films and to map strategy for this week's game. He therefore suggested that the department skim through the rest of the agenda to see whether anybody had anything that couldn't hold until next month.

Since the proposed party for the real estate department, tentatively to be called "Perversionary Interests," was not scheduled to close for six months anyway, it was carried over to the next month's agenda. The discussion of hiring five lateral attorneys for the real estate department was likewise kicked over a month on the theory that the need would be greater in another month and, therefore, the committee's argument could be put more forcefully to the Executive Committee. It was agreed that discussion of whether the department's two paralegals should be granted a raise could also hold, since, if past experience was any guide, both of them would have resigned by next month, in any case.

The Chair never got to ask the committee members whether they felt that the final item on the agenda could be held for another month, because the committee was thrown out bodily by the firm football team. The item was "How to enhance the prestige and power of the real estate department at FWS."

Unconscious, But Productive

While some departments, like Real Estate, have floundered, others, born of necessity, have enjoyed surprising success.

"Look at them, aren't they cute when they sleep?" asked Seymour Plain's secretary, Frieda Jennicks, of her friend, Colleen Moore, as the two brought in lunch and set it on the conference table.

"Well, who are they? And what are they doing here?" asked Colleen.

"It's a long story, Colleen. There's no time to tell it now. Look, they're stirring. It's 12:30; I'm supposed to wake my boss now. Maybe we could just hide in the closet and watch them. That way you can learn firsthand what they're up to."

Awakened gently by Frieda's shake of his shoulders, Seymour stretched and nudged Rebecca Avridge, who was seated on his right. Rebecca shook her head, yawned and nudged Hank LaPlacca, who did the same to Penelope Pincher. Penelope slapped herself gently on both cheeks, stretched and woke Fred Jones.

Chairman Plain started, "I trust all of you committee members have had a pleasant doze, but it's now time for COMA to come to order."

"COMA?" whispered Colleen.

"That's right, the Committee on Mundane Activities," Frieda explained quietly. "It's supposed to be the only committee of its type in the country. COMA was formed to do everything that the other lawyers here at FWS didn't want to do."

"Today's meeting marks the first anniversary of our committee's formation, and I thought we'd devote it to a discussion of how the year has gone," said Chairman

Plain. "Becky, why don't you start by commenting on how recruitment went this year for our area of practice."

"Hiring went much better than any of us could have dreamt," reported Rebecca. "In fact, we bagged more than our quota at every law school at which we interviewed."

"Even at the elite schools, like Harvard and Yale?" LaPlacca asked in disbelief.

"Yup, believe it or not, we found us a mortal Yalie."

"Any notion why the success?" asked LaPlacca.

"Sure, the competition wasn't very tough."

"But the other departments found that the competition was tougher than ever this year," replied LaPlacca.

"Well, our area of the firm's practice has the best of all possible worlds, recruitment-wise. On the one hand, we have the prestige of the firm going for us, and on the other we have a type of practice that most top law students perceive is below them. So we recruit among the next tier of students, who are thrilled to have a chance to work for a firm like ours and who aren't wined and dined by our competitors."

"But what do you tell them when they ask questions about the mundane nature of our work?" asked Jones.

"Most of them don't ask. All they want is a job, any job. But to those who do, I just tell the truth. I tell them that most of the work lawyers do is mundane. The difference between our department and what the students will encounter elsewhere is that we admit it. Most of the students find that candor very refreshing."

"We've had a lot of good comments from young associates who have worked in our area this year," offered Penelope. "They seem to like the fact that things get done."

"What do you mean 'things get done' ?" asked Fred.

"Well, if you get into something like litigation, it seems that things never end. By the time you finish with all the depositions, interrogatories, motions to dismiss and the like, you almost forget what you wanted in the first place. But if your goal is just to draft some bylaws, or photocopy the answers to some interrogatories or cite check a brief, once it's done, it's done. Our associates have found that it gives them a real sense of satisfaction."

"Don't they miss the thrill and challenge of major litigation and multimillion-dollar corporate deals?" asked Jones.

"Oh, some do, I guess. But lately, I've noticed that lawyers from other areas of our practice have been trying to switch into our department," observed LaPlacca. "Some of them are beginning to feel that the regular hours we are able to work in COMA may just compensate for missing some of the challenging legal problems that other departments claim to have."

"They don't even object to making a little less money than some of the big hitters. They've learned that living like a prince instead of a sultan is tolerable," added Plain.

"We are getting some flack from the paralegals, though," Jones commented.

"Yeah, they think that we're horning in on their territory," Pincher agreed.

"So what! They horned in on our territory to begin with," replied Avridge. "Turnabout is fair play. Let them start doing some of the so-called interesting work and stay down until all hours of the evening and work on weekends. Why should we go through three years of law school in order to give them the cushy jobs?"

"Even some of the most senior partners have been scrapping to get into our department lately," said LaPlacca.

"Anybody know why?" asked Pincher.

"Well, I asked Oscar Winters and he told me that some of the older lawyers have found that COMA is the closest thing to practicing law the way they used to. Before all of the esoteric statutes were passed, lawyers were generalists. Now, in the mundane department, we've started to get back to that. Our mundane specialists have a general familiarity with the routine aspects of all the different areas of the law, just the way lawyers used to."

"Even clients seem to love us," added Plain. "One of them told me the other day that we're the only lawyers around the firm who don't create more problems than they solve. And he actually paid our last bill within 120 days."

"The morale of our area seems to be terrific, too," noted Avridge, "especially since, with COMA, we've now got our own committee and recognized specialty. And since we are basically a non-competitive group, we all get along well and pitch in with what needs to be done. There's nothing wrong with the law or lawyers that a little mundanity couldn't cure."

"Damn right," Jones added enthusiastically. "Some day we mundane specialists will be recognized for what we are: the only real lawyers. They'll build a Mundane Lawyers Hall of Fame. I can see it right now, in Catasqua, Pa., midway between the Baseball Hall of Fame in Cooperstown and the Football Hall of Fame in Youngstown. A beautiful shrine, up on a hilltop, a perfect replica of the Supreme Court Building. I can see my plaque in there now, taking its rightful place among the other greats of the profession, the outstanding compilation makers, title searchers, bylaw drafters and interrogatory answerers of our time."

"Is this for real?" Colleen asked Frieda in the closet.

"Of course, honey; mundanity doesn't eliminate grandiosity," replied Frieda.

Over time, COMA came to be the most popular and prestigious department in the firm. People in all specialty areas admired the breadth of their knowledge. Other lawyers admired COMA lawyers' ability to keep their work within manageable bounds and to conduct a life outside of the law. And before long, lawyers in the firm came to see the work done by COMA as interesting work, work that accomplished something concrete rather than the abstract discussions of other specialists, which led nowhere. And all of this was not so very surprising. For interest, like prestige, is in the eyes of the beholder.

Fortunately, Chairman Plain had the foresight to

preserve his domain. Fearing that his partners would get wind of what a content group COMA was, and move to disband it, Plain generated some artificial in-fighting, jockeying for position and bitching about the workload among COMA members. In that way, they appeared to mirror the rest of the firm—and so were left to fend for themselves.

RECRUITMENT

Introduction

Of course, for our firm to continue to grow, we needed bodies to churn out the work that our marketing efforts were spawning. We never used to call them "bodies" when we hired just a few new lawyers each year. In those days, we could afford to pay attention to the individuals we were hiring, and whether they "fit" into our firm. Frankly, now I'm not sure whether nobody fits our firm—or everybody does. Either thought is a little disturbing if you pause to reflect on it, which I try my best not to do too often.

As we and other large firms grew dramatically, the competition for top legal talent became intense. Come to think of it, the competition for mediocre legal talent became intense, too. And that led to foolishness, to recruiting techniques which made law students think that they were coming to a camp rather than a business. We were also forced to look increasingly to the lateral market to hire experienced attorneys—who had bombed out at other firms—to fill the gaping holes left by defections in our own associate ranks. For the privilege of trading failures with our competitors, we paid lofty bounties to headhunters, who photocopied associate resumés at random and sent them to us.

This section chronicles our never-ending efforts to fuel the fires of our firm's growth with fresh kindling.

This Will Hurt You More Than It Hurts Us

After spending countless hours each fall catering to every whim of scores of snotty-nosed law students from coast to coast, it is always dismaying for the Fairweather, Winters & Sommers Hiring Committee, as the December 15 decision day approaches, to receive the inevitable flood of letters from law students around the country rejecting FWS offers. Recently, Stanley Fairweather received a note from one of the upstarts with whom he'd passed an excruciating twenty minutes earlier in the fall.

December 18, 1989

Dear Mr. Fairweather:

It is with regret extraordinaire that I inform you that I will be unable to accept your gracious offer of a summer clerkship with your firm. It was an extremely difficult and heart-wrenching decision for me to make, particularly when I considered the highly impressive attorneys and genuinely pleasant atmosphere that prevailed at your firm. Frankly, though, I got a much better deal elsewhere.

I thank you again for your kind offer. Also, please thank Ms. Rusho-Cruter, who was extremely helpful to me. I would hope that if, for some reason, I decide not to return for permanent employment to the firm I clerk for this summer that you would again consider my application.

Best of luck in your recruiting endeavors and warm wishes for a joyous holiday season.

With high respect,

R.E. Jection

Mr. Fairweather forwarded the letter to the Hiring Committee which, in a fit of pique, retaliated by drafting the following letter for Mr. Fairweather's signature.

December 21, 1989

Dear Mr. Jection:

Yours of the 18th, which I circulated among members
of the Hiring Committee, evoked reactions ranging from
extreme relief to almost uncontrollable giggling. To be perfectly candid(e), your letter gave all of us renewed faith
that this is, indeed, the best of all possible worlds.

You may not have realized just how correct you were
when you said that you were "unable to accept" our offer
at the time you wrote the letter. As you know, our offer
expired at the stroke of midnight on December 15, the
time when the National Association for Law Placement
has decreed that all highly-recruited potential lawyers
turn back into ordinary law student bumpkins. Since your
letter was dated three days after that magic date, even if
you'd been giving us "good news," we would have had some
bad news for you. A tad more attention to your contracts
course might have stood you in good stead.

For future reference, we want you to know that we
truly don't care a fig how tough your decision was. We do,
however, take at face value your representation that this
was, in fact, an extremely difficult decision for you. This
seems to have been verified empirically beyond any
reasonable doubt by your incessant phone calls (collect) to
every member of the Hiring Committee and by your six
visits to the firm subsequent to your original call-back
interview (Ms. Rusho-Cruter, by the way, says that if she
ever sees your puss around our firm again, she will feed
you to the firm's paper shredder).

The difficulty that you have had in making your
decision and your gutless method of writing, rather than

calling us with your news, suggest that your prospects of becoming a takecharge lawyer are not brilliant. Further evidence of this was your confiding to one of our associates on your fifth visit to the firm that thinking about your decision was causing you migraine headaches and periodic vomiting.

You may, perhaps, gain some modicum of solace in knowing that our own decision on whether to extend an offer to you was deadlocked until, on the 23rd ballot, a member of the committee suggested that the matter be resolved by horse-and-goggling. You won, as a rock breaks a scissors.

Nor, frankly, Mr. Jection, do we care that you found our attorneys impressive and our atmosphere pleasant. We've been wowing law students for decades and, in all candor, have found that it's not that tough to impress a second-year law student, even a pseudo-sophisticate like yourself. And though our atmosphere may well have seemed pleasant to you in short snatches, we feel sure as God made little green apples that you would have found it oppressive in the long haul; certainly, most of us do, but we put up with it because the money's good.

We do congratulate you on your establishment of a new firm interviewee record, having milked the firm for seven lunches, four dinners and three all-expenses paid trips to Chicago for you and your "significant other." (In this regard, you may be interested to know that your wife of five years has expressed some chagrin at your constant reference to her as a "significant other.")

Our experience with you has caused us to rethink our wining and dining policy and to revamp it in a manner that makes it virtually impossible that your record will be exceeded. Accordingly, we have bronzed your expense reimbursement slips and placed them in our Interviewee Hall of Fame along with other hiring memorabilia, such as the 17-page resume of I. M. Spectackler, the fold-out color picture of Gretta Lodammee and the rejection letter we wrote to Louis Dembitz Brandeis.

As to your hope that we would consider your application again should you submit one next year, we would encourage you to do so. In fairness, however, I should disclose that it is the present consensus among committee members that it will be an extremely nippy day in hell before we would invite you in for more interviews with us. I am encouraging your reapplication, however, as several committee members would experience more than moderate satisfaction in turning you down cold.

Mr. Jection, we appreciate your having agonized over this decision and recognize that you must have fantasized over the anguish we would feel at your rejection letter. You should know, however, that we put out offers to so many second-year law students that, by the time they accept or reject our offers, we generally don't even remember who they are, or why we made offers to them in the first place.

We hope that you have a gala summer at your chosen firm and that you don't screw up so badly that you are forced to come groveling back to us next fall.

Good tidings of comfort and joy, comfort and joy.

Very truly yours,

Stanley J. Fairweather

Summer Romance

To: All Lawyers
From: Hiring Committee

It's no secret that our last three summer programs have not gone entirely tickety-boo. And though it's undoubtedly true that numbers, as replevin, may lie, certain statistics admit only grudgingly of more than one interpretation. The chart below sets forth the grizzliest of the figures that emerge from our recent hiring experience:

Summer of	Students Hired for Summer	Offers Made to Students	Offers to Summer Students	Acceptances
1985	10	15	9	7
1986	12	25	8	6
1987	15	40	7	3
1988	17	82	16	2
1989	21	314	18	1

From this table, certain facts fairly slap one in the face. The number of students hired for the summer of 1986 is two-thirds the number of offers made to students after the summer of 1989. The number of students hired in 1987 is precisely equal to the number of offers made to hire students in 1985. The number of students hired for the summer of 1986, plus the number of offers made to attract students in 1985, is equal to the number of offers made after the summer of 1985 times the number of acceptances after the summer of 1987, and both are only slightly greater than twenty-six. And 314 is equal to the sum of all the other numbers in the table.

Now, my friends, we can choose to ignore these numbers; we can bury our heads in the proverbial sand; we can put our hands over our eyes and whistle "Dixie" or "La Donna è Mobile;" we can fiddle while Rome burns or combine some or all of the above (though I don't recommend whistling anything while your head is buried in the sand). But neither these reactions, nor great Neptune's oceans, can wash away these numbers. To resort to any of these diversions would be to treat the symptom, not the disease, or to shoot the messenger who bears bad tidings or to lock the barn door after the horse has gotten out. What is called for is a drastic change in our summer program. We've got to give these kids what they want, send the little bastards back to their law schools with something to talk about. To that end, your Hiring Committee has developed the plan set forth below, under Below, for next summer.

Below

Initial impact can be so important. Too many firms wait for as long as a week to throw a lavish party for a student after he or she arrives. What kind of treatment is that, huh? Will that student feel loved and wanted? Nyet!

This year, Ms. Rusho-Cruter, our recruitment coordinator, will circulate lists of the arrival times of summer clerks. Twenty-five lawyers will be assigned to ride out to O'Hare, in a bus chartered for that purpose, to greet each new student. A high-school marching band will strike up "The Battle Hymn (or Person) of the Republic" as the student deplanes, and lawyers from the firm will display placards ranging from "Fairweather, Winters & Sommers Welcomes You" to "No Nukes." The law student will be hoisted to the shoulders of the Fairweather group and carried through the diverse religious groups that inhabit the airport, with the high-school band leading the way blaring the theme song from *L. A. Law.*

On then, via private limousine, to the Fairweather offices, where, in the firm's spiffiest conference room, the entire Executive Committee of Fairweather, Winters & Sommers rises, as one, to applaud the summer student's entry. Stanley Fairweather, founder of the firm, delivers the welcoming panegyric:

"On behalf of the entire prestigious and historic law firm of Fairweather, Winters & Sommers: 'Hi.' Each and every one of us, even down to the least significant little associate, is just pleased as punch, or more so, that you have decided to pass this summer with us. Well aware are we of how fortunate we are to have snared you. All of us on the Executive Committee have reviewed your credentials, and to say that we are in awe of your accomplishments would be to understate that which we are in of them. *Who's Who in American Colleges and Universities,* American Jurisprudence Book Award in Legal Profession, member of the student bar association, varsity high-school letter in badminton, interests as diverse as philately and jogging, you are a veritable twentieth-century da Vinci. Full well do we know that you had your pick of firms, and to think that you chose us, well, frankly, it's almost too providential to contemplate. (Note: here the entire Executive Committee rises to warble the Hallelujah chorus from Handel's "Messiah.") As I approach my middle dotage, it is the thought that this firm will be perpetuated, and my retirement benefits assured, by the likes of you that paints this shit-eating grin on my face. In short, my lucky stars are frequently what I thank when we attract somebody of your caliber.

"We'd like to present you with a few small gifts to start you on your way. First, these keys are to the brand new fire-red Porsche that is parked right outside. Yours for the summer; should you decide to join us as an associate, you can drive it back to school as your own. Next, these keys will open the door of your rent-free Gold Coast duplex condominium, where your private chef, Luigi, personal valet, Sid, and housekeeper, Bridget, are waiting to attend your every whim. Guest memberships have been reserved in your name at three of the most exclusive clubs in the Chicagoland area and, of course, any charges that you may run up there will be billed directly to and paid

for by the firm. Now, you've had an exhausting day, I know, so why not drive on home. If there's anything that any of us on the E.C. can do for you during the course of the summer, just give us a tinkle."

While this should provide a suitable kickoff, we will have to continue to pamper the little prima donnas with, *inter alia,* lunches, dinners, and parties as the summer progresses. Your attitude will be an important influence on whether these students return to us. Remember at all times that practicing law is fun at Fairweather, Winters & Sommers (a weekly memorandum will be circulated to all lawyers during the summer to remind them of this). Pay a lot of personal attention to the summer students. Invite them for cocktails. If your place is not sufficiently opulent, get your parents' or a friend's pad for the evening. The firm has arranged with the Art Institute to permit you to decorate your home by borrowing major works of art on an overnight basis.

To assure an interesting work mix for the summer, your Hiring Committee has made up legal problems to distribute to summer clerks and has hired a troupe of gypsy thespians to serve as clients. Thus, by summer's end each clerk will have had his or her own larger-than-life first amendment experience, tender offer battle, securities registration and real estate acquisition. While this approach admittedly is not altogether honest, it should be effective.

All summer clerks crave feedback and we intend to assure that they get it. In feedingback, lawyers should be flattering, but not obsequious. Thus, it is appropriate to say, "This is one of the finest jobs ever produced by a summer clerk at this or any other prestigious firm." But lawyers should avoid, "This memo combines the legal craftspersonship of Brandeis, Cardozo and Cosell with the literary style of Dostoevsky, Hemingway and Seuss. It is compelling. I read it in a single sitting. Certain to be a Memo-of-the-Month Club selection, it heralds the arrival on the American scene of a great new memo writer. It is one of the most important first memos of the decade."

Of course, the making or non-making of a successful summer program depends ultimately on how many offers are extended to summer clerks. Because a failure to extend an offer can sabotage our recruiting efforts nationwide for several years, your Hiring Committee has determined to accede to the blackmail and to extend permanent offers to all summer clerks, regardless of the quality of their work. This should markedly enhance our attractiveness to law students, without significantly affecting the quality of the people we hire.

Your Hiring Committee recognizes that the program outlined above is not exactly what most lawyers now at the firm experienced. It is thus natural that many of you will resent this kow-towing to the kiddie corps. To this your Hiring Committee counsels patience. Wait 'til we get the little bastards as associates!

Sommers Camp

Once again, last summer the best laid plans of the FWS Hiring Committee went awry. Eight of the summer associates sent to Europe on SAP (Summer Abroad Program) were captured by terrorists and held captive for two months. Eventually, the Executive Committee was forced to cough up $2,000,000 in ransom, after the terrorists rejected Stanley Fairweather's offer to substitute Nails Nuttree for the summer associate hostages. Under stern orders from the Executive Committee to change their game next year, the Hiring Committee circulated this memo.

To: **All Partners**
From: **Rex Gladhand, Hiring Committee Chair**

The Hiring Committee has determined that our entire approach to next year's summer program will be changed. In the past, we have spent a tremendous amount of lawyer time and money in interviewing at more than twenty law schools and bringing interviewees in to wine and dine them. And we have spent an enormous amount of money on salaries and entertainment during the summer.

We have been forced to deal with increasingly restrictive law school interview rules. The schools tell us whom we must interview, when we must interview, what we may and may not ask interviewees and how long we must keep our offers open.

We have faced an increased risk of being sued for equal opportunity employment violations. We have been forced to provide highly paid law students a potpourri of extracurricular activities at the firm's expense.

Frankly, we're sick of it.

Next year's program will involve no interviewing of law students either at the law school or the firm, and no salary to law students during the summer. Next year, Fairweather, Winters & Sommers, always in the vanguard of law firm reform and improvement, will institute, as its summer program, Sommers Camp.

Akin to the development of other specialty camps such as music camps, sports camps and tripping camps, Sommers Camp will be a law camp. Recruiting will be done by sending the parents of law students a slick brochure urging them to send their kids to enjoy a summer in the pure high-altitude air, amidst the office greenery of Sommers Camp. The brochure has not yet gone to press, but a preliminary draft contains the following information:

➤ The camp will be available as an overnight camp for second-year law students and as a day camp for the younger, less mature first-year students, who would otherwise be likely to suffer homesickness.

➤ The fee payable to Sommers Camp will be $19,995 for the overnight program and $14,995 for the day camp. (Parents with two children in the program will receive their choice of an eight percent reduction in price or a free pour-over will with marital trust.) Campers wishing to split their summers will pay the full fee, plus 10%.

➤ This camp is for rough and ready types, not sissies. For example, there will be an early survival training program in which new campers will be brought into the firm blindfolded, spun around three times and required to find the vending machine room; there will be a canoe trip down the scenic Chicago River, with an overnight at the printer.

➤ Parents will be kept informed. Campers will be required to dictate at least two letters home a week; the personnel counselors will give parents a mid-summer review and a full report on their child's development at the end of the summer; parents will be permitted to visit campers on Visiting Day.

➤ Instead of expensive meals at fancy restaurants at firm expense, the fare will be sandwiches from the Mahzel Deli and weenie roasts in the conference rooms.

➤ Campers will be taught discipline. Offices will be inspected each morning by Colonel Hargraves (campers who do not pass inspection will not receive their nightly treat, a photocopy of a Baby Ruth bar); campers will be required to wear neat, clean camp uniforms (three-piece suits for both boys and girls); when the receptionist calls "buddies" over the paging system, campers will be required to find their buddies (this system has been instituted for safety reasons, since we have lost a number of students in past summers).

➤ There will be ample opportunity for fun: at weekly cocktail parties, at the big firm party bash, and at an evening comedy show (campers will also be invited to attend a real partnership meeting).

➤ The most important part of the summer will be the intensive legal training that the campers will receive: Assignments will be made by our assignment chief, John Runningchild; training will be done by such skilled experts in their field as Chief Dying

Horse on "How Not to Avoid Probate," and Chief Taxing Voidance on "Sections 722(b), 137, 98, 532(c)(8), 1273(a), 807, 8(d)(5), and 422 of the Internal Revenue Code, and why they have no relationship to one another;" worthy campers will be inducted into the Benevolent and Protective Order of the Memo (BPOM), the camp honorary society.

If you have any questions or suggestions, of if you happen to know the addresses of the parents of any law students, please contact me or any member of the Hiring Committee.

Hiring Wars

The Fairweather Winters & Sommers Hiring Committee was wrestling with a difficult problem at its annual post-Labor Day meeting to kick off the hiring season. Last fall, they had fallen short of the body count dictated by the Executive Committee in hiring second-year students. Way short. Instead of twenty, the Hiring Committee had been able to muster up only ten. There seemed little chance indeed that they would be able to hire the twenty-five new associates the Executive Committee had ordered for next fall.

"There's no use crying about our situation. What we need is a solution," advised Rex Gladhand.

"What would make our firm more attractive to law students? That's the question," offered Vance Winkle.

"How about more money?" suggested Heather Regale.

"Great idea, Heather. Can't you just see our Executive Committee doing cartwheels over how clever we were to come up with that one? I assume you saw the memo they just circulated about cutting down on the number of pencils we use, to try to cut costs," said Alex Pouts.

"What about increasing the amount we put into our

pension plan? That would have the benefit of keeping associates around for several years, since it doesn't vest for three years," said Lionel Hartz.

"Trouble with that is law students have a time horizon of about forty minutes. None of them expects to be around after three years, so a pension would not be much of a selling point," argued Rex.

"Maybe we just need to recruit better," Vance suggested, "have our senior partners pay more attention to the students."

"Have you taken a look at our senior partners lately, Vance? If you think we've got problems now, all we'd have to do is turn Oscar Winters loose on the law students and you'd see real problems."

"You've got a point, Rex," Vance admitted. "What if we give our younger associates a bigger budget to wine and dine the students?"

"I put my foot down there," said Alex. "By the time the hiring season is over, those spoiled brats have eaten at Le Perroquet more than I have in twenty years."

"Maybe we're taking the wrong tack in thinking about what we could do to make ourselves more attractive to law students," said Gerald Forspiel.

"What the hell are you talking about, Gerry?" asked Alex.

"Well, here's my thought. Why are we losing students? Because other firms, particularly Shirkland & Malice, are more attractive than we are—right?"

"Right, but I still don't get it," said Alex.

"Bear with me. There are two ways to make us more attractive, relative to the Shirkland firm. We can either make us more attractive or make them less attractive to the students we want."

"If you're suggesting that we bad-mouth the Shirkland firm, forget it. We all have good friends over there. And if we got into a bad-mouthing contest, we'd lose—they've got more on us than we could ever get on them," said Lionel.

"Bad-mouth Shirkland? Perish the thought. I'm surprised that you'd imagine I would suggest such a thing."

"Then what *are* you suggesting?" asked Alex, annoyed.

"The problem, as I see it, is that we are both trying to attract the same students. If they were to recruit different students than our firm, we wouldn't be in competition."

"Yes, and if I were two feet taller, I'd be 7-3," said Heather. "You're not making sense. Shirkland is not going to all of a sudden stop recruiting the same top students that we go after."

"Not voluntarily," said Gerry, with a smile.

"You really are crazy. How are we going to make them stop recruiting students involuntarily?"

"Simple. When a Hiring Committee member goes to interview at a law school, what does he do? He comes back, gives the recruitment office a list of those he wants to invite back and those he wants to reject. They feed the list into the word processor and it belches out offer and rejection letters. Now, if their computer were to make an error and accidentally reject all of those they intended to make offers to, why, I'll bet that we wouldn't be in competition for many of the same students."

"Gerald, you wicked boy you! But how would we make that accident happen?" asked Heather.

"Nothing easier. Firms need word-processing talent almost as badly as they need ERISA lawyers. All we do is have one of our word-processing operators go over to Shirkland, apply for a job and then have a little accident."

"I think your suggestion is unconscionable and unethical—let's do it," Heather said enthusiastically.

Postscript

Gerald's plan was a modified success. The Fairweather firm lost only one student to Shirkland that year. But the firm of Mayer, Green & Flat knocked the hell out of them. And of the fourteen students hired accidentally by Shirkland that year, twelve became partners in the firm. The other two are federal judges.

Making Womb for More Lawyers

The hiring season was grinding to a halt and the Hiring Committee had not bagged its limit. In fact, with Thanksgiving just around the corner, they had fallen 21 short of the 25 bodies they had hoped to hire for the next season, despite the efforts they'd made to sabotage the Shirkland recruiting efforts by gaining control of their word-processing operation. There would be hell to pay when the committee reported at the next partnership meeting.

Chairman Rex Gladhand asked if there were any suggestions.

Alex Pouts suggested that the whole thing might be blamed on a disastrous summer program. And, he added, "that article in the October *All-American Lawyer,* likening our firm atmosphere to 'a sort of latter day Spanish Inquisition' didn't exactly help at the law schools either." The other committee members pointed out two problems with that. Since their committee was responsible for the summer program, they could hardly escape criticism for their failure to hire by pointing to their summer program failures. Furthermore, for the last three years, the firm had been panned by *The All-American Lawyer* and it actually had helped the recruitment effort because of the esteem in which that publication is held by the more savvy law students around the country.

Lionel Hartz suggested that it was not too late to avoid facing the music. The committee could dash out quickly to a nearby law school and hire a bunch of turkeys before Thanksgiving to make the committee's performance look more respectable. Then, a year later, when the turkeys had to be canned, the Personnel Committee would be left holding the bag.

Alex Pouts next suggested blaming the failure on the associates at the firm, for telling too many of the interviewees the truth about the firm.

Hartz agreed that a scapegoat was needed, but did not favor putting the onus on the associates. "After all, we've got to depend on those little bastards to grind out the work and, if we give them a bum rap on the hiring thing, they'll get even with us in some other way. I think that the only honorable thing to do is to blame the person whose sole responsibility is hiring: our recruitment coordinator, Rose Rusho-Cruter. Why not just can her?"

Vance Winkle thought that there were at least two very cogent reasons not to can Rose. First, the firm would not even have hired the four that they did, except for her. And second, and more important, from sitting in on committee meetings, Rose knew enough dirt to scuttle the firm's next five years' hiring efforts.

Heather Regale pointed out that the committee could always fall back on some of their old standard excuses: the competition is getting tougher as employers are hiring larger numbers of students from the same pool, the firm was unwilling to spend what it took to wine and dine the young whippersnappers, etc. Or it could resort to the old trick of counting in this year's total people who were hired during the middle of the year or were hired the previous year and took the year off to clerk.

Rex said that he thought the committee had pretty well covered the ground as to the possible explanations and that they had better turn to thinking about what they might do to improve the take next season.

Suddenly, Hank LaPlacca, a new committee member who had remained silent throughout the meeting piped up, "Begging your pardon, fellow members, may a rookie have the floor?" Rex said that of course Hank could have the floor and, on appeal of Rex's ruling, he was sustained, 4-3.

"When I was in college, I was a history major," started Hank, whereupon one member who had voted in the majority on the previous question asked if it was too late to change his vote and was told by Rex that it was. "Anyway, as I was saying," repeated Hank, "I was a history major in college. That perspective has always caused me to take the long view of things and I think that we, on the Hiring Committee, should have our eye on the long term.

"While it is fine to discuss minor tamperings with our procedure for the small and temporary relief that they may bring in the short haul, they are not likely to solve our problems. As I see it, the push is to get students committed to the firm at younger and younger ages. For the last few years, we have been employing first-year law students with great success. I think that we have got to push the barriers back even further."

"You are not suggesting that we start hiring seniors in college for heaven sakes, are you?" asked Rex.

"No, I am suggesting that we go back even further, much further, in fact. With the tight economy, parents will be pushing their children into career paths earlier and earlier, and with the cost of education soaring, I don't see why we can't start picking out some really top prospects in kindergarten and grooming them for a place at our firm. The parents would agree to commit them to working at our firm and we, in turn, would bear the cost of the education of these tots and offer them summer employment."

"That's ridiculous, Hank. You want to hire a bunch of kids for the summer who aren't even toilet trained?"

"No, we could ask them in the interview at kindergarten whether they are pottie trained."

"Oh, no, we couldn't," objected Heather. "To ask that question would run afoul of the rules of the National Association for Law Placement, which prohibit discrimination based upon hygienic development. We'd be banned from interviewing at all of the major law schools."

"Any more bright ideas, Hank?" asked Alex.

"Well, as a matter of fact, I did have another idea. But I suppose that, given your reaction to my kindergarten idea, you're not likely to be too receptive to this one either."

"Give us a chance, Hank, what is it?"

"I think that we ought to abolish our no nepotism rule."

"Why is that going to help our hiring situation? All that will do is to make a few more people potentially eligible for a position with the firm."

"Well, abolishing the nepotism rule is only a part of my plan. Once it's abolished, I think that we ought to marshal our resources and start to breed lawyers for the firm. If we need a litigator, we get one of our most talented litigators and mate him or her with some good stock. In another twenty-four years or so, you've got yourself one hell of a little litigator. Naturally, after a while, we will get into some more sophisticated crossbreeding. So, for example, if you have some good litigator genes, but want to tone down the spirit, you might mate the person with a real estate lawyer. Some problems are likely to remain, however. For example, it will be impossible to get a purebred ERISA lawyer, since when you put two ERISA lawyers together, they haven't the necessary combined energy to mate.

"Once we have filled our firm's present and future needs, we can use the same techniques to bring in substantial additional revenue for the firm. Can you imagine the stud fees that a lawyer of Stan Fairweather's caliber would fetch?"

It's For Your Own Good

In order to attract top law students, it's not enough to pay
them far more than they're worth and give them challenging
work for major clients. No, some students want to make sure
that the firm is doing good while it does well. The FWS Pro
Bono Publico Committee is the firm's attempt to lure do-good
law students into their lair. Here's an account of a recent
meeting of that committee.

The FWS Pro Bono Publico Committee held its monthly
luncheon meeting in the Napoleon Room of the exclusive Bigwig Club, which admits no women, Jews,
blacks, Hispanics or near-sighted persons. Committee
members in the foregoing categories maintained contact
with committee deliberations from a phone booth outside.

Hardly had the meeting been summoned to order by
its chairman, Rodriguez Hiram-Betty (whose wife and he
had spurned the trendy hyphenation of last names by instead hyphenating their middle names), when a club
employee interrupted to announce that there was an important call for Mr. Hiram-Betty.

Rod returned and reported that the call had been
from Rachel Steinberg, phoning from the booth outside, to
raise, on behalf of those committee members excluded
from the Bigwig Club, the question of whether future
meetings might be moved to another situs. Steinberg had
been selected by the outcasts as their mouthpiece since,
being near of sight, she was the only committee member
excluded from the Bigwig Club on three grounds.

There ensued a discussion of the outcasts' request.
Mr. Percifal Snikkety objected that the request, not
having been raised by somebody physically present at the
meeting, was not properly before the committee. The
Chair overruled the objection, noting that he was raising
the matter and he was here, large as life.

Snikkety then suggested, respectfully, that the Chair lacked standing to raise the matter, since he had not been excluded from the Bigwig Club. But the Chair squelched that objection because the club had attempted to oust him when he'd changed his first name to Rodriguez, "and that was good enough."

Freed at last of procedural shackles, the debate plunged headlong to the merits of switching the situs of future meetings. Patrick Conshenz, a new committee member, thought this a capital opportunity to make a symbolic statement against discriminatory policies, adding that it also would be "sorta nice" to have the whole committee together in one room. Concurring in the conclusion, though not in the reasoning, Alex Pouts backed the situs switch on the ground that lunch at the club had, of late, become too dear.

Tu quoque, Snikkety argued that the Bigwig Club served irrefragably the best meals in town and that it would, therefore, be a far, far better thing to do to remain at the club and to labor for change in the discriminatory club rules from within. Here, another club employee barged in to inform the Chair that Ms. Steinberg, on behalf of the outcasts, had rung up again to beseech committee members to speak more loudly, as the boothlings were having trouble hearing, what with the heavy noontime traffic whizzing by the phone booth.

As debate resumed, Snikkety, bedding at long last a fear that was nagging nobody, opined brashly that he perceived no constitutional impediment to the committee continuing to meet in a club that discriminates. And, he added somewhat less loftily, several top execs of prime FWS clients were Bigwig officers who might not warm to the committee switching its meeting place.

As the dover sole almondine in a light sauterne sauce was ushered in, one member flapped the group's memory that Oscar Winters had been a founding Bigwig. Thereupon, those present voted unanimously to continue meeting at the club, but to work, *sub silento* and *incognito,* for glacial change from within.

After lunch, the meeting resumed to noodle over whether the firm, *qua* firm, should take a position on proposals being floated by pinkos at the American Bar Association that would require every lawyer to donate time to providing pro bono legal services. Extended discussion of this issue was obviated when it was reported that the organized bar, bulwarks of progressive thought that they are, had been so repulsed by the notion of being compelled to provide minimal services to those who most needed them that mandatory pro bono had already been junked by the ABA, and the original proposer had been exiled to Omaha.

Up next, agenda-wise, were requests for firm contributions from eight charitable organizations. It was moved and seconded that all such requests be denied. Conshenz asked whether it would be okay to read the names of the organizations that had requested contributions. Snikkety objected that reading the names would create a dangerous precedent, since it would imply that the identity of the charity was relevant, which it wasn't, given the firm's policy of not making any contributions.

Conshenz inquired as to what the thinking had been in adopting the policy, since it seemed contrary to the generous giving practice of many corporations. Snikkety explained that while corporations were merely squandering shareholder money, a firm contribution would be taking bread off partners' tables. Though the firm's ironclad non-contribution policy was dented occasionally to permit beneficence towards pet charities or political candidates of key clients, Stan Fairweather had pronounced this copacetic and, therefore, consistent with firm policy.

There being no further discussion, the motion to ignore all contribution requests carried unanimously. Club employees now circulated with port, cognac and cigars, and the discussion turned to what new pro bono cases the firm should take on. At the request of Conshenz, the Chairman reviewed the docket of pending pro bono matters:

> *Proudhorn v. Proudhorn*—divorce case; FWS client is Phineas Proudhorn, Stanley J. Fairweather's chauffeur.

> *State v. Proudhorn*—speeding ticket; FWS client is Phineas Proudhorn, who was apprehended shortly after Mr. Fairweather's admonition to "Step on it, you dolt, or I'll miss my tee-off time."

> *Mary Doe v. Proudhorn*—paternity suit; FWS client is Phineas Proudhorn; alleged wrongdoing occurred on Proudhorn's day off, in the back seat of Stanley Fairweather's El Dorado, and forms part of the basis of the divorce suit, *supra.*

> Parakeets for Peace, Inc.—not-for-profit corporation formed by FWS at the beck of the senior vice-president of a large corporate client; part of an international string of organizations (in Australia, "Budgies Against Belligerence") dedicated to promoting world peace by teaching pet birds to sing, "We Ain'ta Gonna Study War No More."

> *Internal Revenue Service v. Parakeets for Peace, Inc.*—defense of IRS suit challenging defendant's tax-exempt status on the ground that the latter discriminates on the basis of sex, since its avowed purpose is to teach parakeets the words to a song and only male parakeets can learn to talk.

> *Honorable C. Wordsworth Coinflip v. The All-American Lawyer*—libel action brought by FWS on behalf of Judge Coinflip of the Circuit Court of Cook County against defendant for

naming him "one of the seven worst judges in state court history," intimating that he'd escaped conviction in the Greyland scandal because prosecutors concluded he was "too stupid to bribe," and suggesting that "a moderately intelligent chimpanzee could write more coherent opinions than Coinflip." (FWS has several important cases before Coinflip that only a chimp could decide in favor of FWS's clients.)

As the Chair finished reviewing the docket, a woebegone club employee entered with tidings that the boothlings had fed their last farthing to Ma Bell and were no longer communicado. Taking note of the lateness of the hour, the Chair suggested, in deference to the severed committee members and in view of the rather oppressive pro bono burden being shouldered by the firm already, that consideration of doing yet more good might be tabled until the next committee meeting, scheduled for noon on All Saints Day.

Slipping Them In, Laterally

There was a time in the not too distant past when lawyer hiring at Fairweather, Winters & Sommers was done by a single committee called, appropriately enough, the Hiring Committee. The Hiring Committee did no lateral hiring. Indeed, the firm liked to boast that it bred its own attorneys. This was possible because the firm grew slowly, some would say excruciatingly so.

Suddenly, though, the firm's business expanded dramatically. Instead of the occasional attorney, the firm required a steady supply of bodies. And an increasing number of bodies began to leave. So the firm was forced to hire laterally.

For quite some time, though, the hiring of a lateral attorney remained an unusual event at FWS, handled on an ad hoc basis by the Hiring Committee. As more and more lateral attorneys were hired, however, and as hiring out of law school expanded as well, the job of the FWS Hiring Committee became overwhelming. In an incredible tactical blunder, Rex Gladhand, Chair of the Hiring Committee, complained about the workload of the committee at a meeting of the Executive Committee. Before he knew what had hit him, his committee was stripped of jurisdiction over lateral hirees.

The Lats, as the Committee on Lateral Hiring is known around the firm, have become a formidable force. They are the only committee, for example, to develop their own logo: an attorney lying prone and wearing a three-piece suit. Members of Lats proudly display the prone attorney on their shirts and sweaters, in lieu of alligators and polo ponies.

Last week, head Lat Alphonse Proust reported to the FWS Executive Committee. "Mr. Chairman, may it please the E.C.," Proust began in his appealing manner, "it gives me a great deal of pleasure to report to you that, since last January, we have bagged seven new laterals, two in tax, two in environmental, one in real estate, one in securities, and one who we're not quite sure what he's doing.

"That concludes my report, and now I would be pleased to answer any appropriate questions. I would like to thank each and every one of you for your attention and I would like to reserve five minutes for rebuttal."

"Al," said Sherman Clayton, "is it true that certain jurisdictional disputes have developed between your committee and the Hiring Committee?"

"Yes, Sherm, there have been a few. For example, both committees are claiming jurisdiction over the hiring of lawyers who have just completed a judicial clerkship or who have obtained an advanced degree, such as an MBA. Furthermore, the Hiring Committee is trying to deny us access to Ms. Rusho-Cruter's services. We ask that this committee act to resolve these disputes."

"Al," said Jane Hokum-Cohen, "this hardly seems like such a major matter that the Executive Committee should spend time on it. Can't your committees resolve this between you? After all, you do have a common goal here."

"We have tried to resolve it peaceably among us, Jane, but we've been unable to do it. We even had a joint meeting to attempt to explore these common problems, but it nearly ended in blows. I think we need your guidance."

"Well," said Jane, "if you can't agree, why not split the difference? I suggest that an Interim Committee on Semi-Laterals be created, its members to be appointed half by the Chair of Lats and half by the Chair of the Hiring Committee, the new committee to have jurisdiction over hiring judicial clerks and students with advanced degrees and the recruitment coordinator to be available to the interim committee, but to speak only with those members of the committee who were appointed by the Chair of the Hiring Committee."

Jane's suggestion was so obviously even-handed and nonsensical that it passed unanimously, without further discussion. Jane was named Chair of the new interim committee.

Phillip D. W. Wilson III, a new member of the E.C., then asked why it was necessary to incur the rather hefty fees to headhunters that had been paid recently by the Lats. Alphonse said that he thought it was necessary to pay these fees in order to hire the headhunters to do for the firm what the firm would not be caught dead doing on its own behalf. "For example, the firm would not itself consider calling lawyers at other firms to see if they would be interested in switching over to FWS, so we hire Bwana Headhunters, Inc., to do it on our behalf."

Phillip said that didn't make a whole lot of sense to him. "Either it is OK to raid other firms, in which case it would be cheaper and more effective for us to do it our-selves, or it isn't, in which case it is improper to hire somebody to do it for us."

"But," said Alphonse, "if FWS raided other firms for younger lawyers, those firms would begin to do the same thing to FWS."

"You mean instead of having Bwana Headhunters, Inc., do it on their behalf, as they do now?" asked Phillip rhetorically.

Al admitted that Phillip seemed to have a point, but assured the committee that the point made only super-ficial sense. Lats had itself considered the matter several times and each time had come to the conclusion that the point Phillip seemed to be making did not, on close analysis, hold much water, although he could not remem-ber exactly why right now.

Several other E.C. members agreed with Al that the type of point Phillip was making was exactly the sort of point that often is silly once you take a lot of time to look into it and that they didn't see why the entire E.C., the most productive group in the firm, should waste a lot of time looking into something that, on close analysis, was likely to prove worthless. The vote to censure P.D.W. Wilson carried, with only P.D.W. Wilson dissenting.

Sherman Clayton asked whether Al had heard rumors that some of the firm's associates were concerned about the extent of the lateral hiring the firm was doing and, if so, what the committee proposed to do about it.

"There can be no question," admitted Al, "that there is concern among the associates about the firm's lateral hiring. Much of this concern has been expressed in unfortunate ways. I think that the picketing of Lats meetings by associates, while perhaps constitutionally protected, is juvenile. Likewise, the spray painting of the hallways with slogans such as 'Lats Go Home' and 'Death to the Capitalist Lat-Pigs' is not calculated to spawn constructive dialogue. Finally, on a purely human level, constant references to the lateral hirees who have come to the firm as 'scabs,' and so-called practical jokes, such as filling their attaché cases with raspberry yogurt, are despicable.

"Recognizing the problem, of course," continued Al, "is not solving it. One approach would be to take a hard line and fire the associates who are being so ugly to the laterals. The problem with that is that such an action would create still more lateral positions to be filled, and the committee is having enough trouble filling the existing vacancies.

"Another tack would be to ignore the problem and hope it goes away. This is the approach the firm takes toward almost every other problem it faces and, since it doesn't work on those problems, we see no reason to suppose that it will work on this one.

"So the Lats have decided to try a subtle and humane approach. We have arranged a series of teas for associates and laterals, at which we hope they will get to know each other. We have also taken to including one-line phrases at the bottom of memos that are circulated to all attorneys— messages such as 'Laterals are people too' and 'Have you hugged a lateral today?' Finally, we have set up an ad hoc Lateral-Associate Matchmaking Committee, known informally as the Yentas, whose purpose it is to encourage intermarriage between laterals and associates in the hope that this will, in the long run, foster greater understanding between the two groups."

The Associate Draft

For years, the law firm of Fairweather Winters & Sommers was dissatisfied with available methods of hiring attorneys laterally. The process was expensive and time-consuming. Unable to locate laterals themselves, the firm was forced to turn to headhunters, who regularly ignored their requirements and charged exorbitant fees for little work. "There must be a better way," thought many on the Lats, the Fairweather Lateral Hiring Committee. And indeed there was.

A few months ago, the National Association for Law Placement, emulating the National Football League and the National Basketball Association, instituted a lateral draft, scheduled to commence in late 1991. Reacting promptly to NALP's announcements, the Fairweather firm created the Committee on Drafting Associates. CODA, the firm's newest and smallest committee, consists of only two members: General Manager Alphonse Proust and Manager Herbert Gander. Here is an account of a pre-draft meeting.

Alphonse called the meeting to order and announced that, if there were no serious objections, he would act as Chair of the meeting. He asked Herb if he would mind acting as secretary. Herb said he would waive minding, if Alphonse would lend him a pencil and a piece of paper on which to take minutes. Alphonse did.

Alphonse noted the presence of a quorum and stated that the meeting was competent to proceed. Herb thanked the chair for the compliment regarding his competence.

The Chair asked the secretary to read the minutes of

the last meeting. The secretary told the Chair he'd forgotten them at home, but would bring them next time, probably.

The meeting waxed meaty. "We've got to make our final decisions, Herb. The lateral draft takes place next Monday. Who do you think we ought to take first?"

"Well, we've got two choices in the first round this year: No. 6 and No. 19. It was smart to trade that corporate paralegal and assistant office manager for another first-round pick. I think we ought to go for a good defensive tax man and maybe an offensive litigator. Come to think of it, that may be redundant. Litigators *are* offensive."

"I don't think we need a tax man; we've got enough."

"Well, you can never tell if we'll lose one."

"We can protect them."

"Protect them?"

"Sure, under the rules that the commissioner of laterals put out, we can protect 20 percent of our associates. That's so the new expansion firms can't gobble them up."

"I don't know, our scouts tell me it's a good year for antitrust lawyers. With the Republicans' pro-business stance, a lot of former trustbusters are pounding the pavement. We could pick us up a couple of good ones cheap, convert 'em to real estate lawyers and, if the Democrats get elected and antitrust comes back into vogue, we got 'em in the bullpen ready to bring in."

"Nope, I don't think so, Alphonse. We've got two of our own antitrusters right now that we're tryin' to unload. One of 'em confided the other day that he was trying to find a place, but he was learning that, in the relevant market, he was irrelevant."

"Well, maybe we ought to take a look at who's available before we decide what departments we're going to stock."

"Good idea; what about this guy: Harvard Law School grad, three years' experience in litigation with a major

Cleveland law firm, looks pretty solid to me. Says he's never lost a case, he's 8-0."

"Naw, he'll probably go early. Besides, anybody who chooses Cleveland may not have the requisite judgment for our firm. And as to his record, do you know any litigators who *have* lost a case? How about this guy; he goes both ways."

"What do you mean by that, Alphonse?"

"Does both litigation and ERISA."

"Are you kidding, he must be schizoid. We've got enough crazies; I say we take a pass."

"Okay, what about this lady: Reasonably decent law school record, law review, and three years at a medium-size firm in Chicago."

"You're right, she looks good. But I don't think we'll have to use a first-round pick on her. She went to a second-tier law school. She'll be around in the second or third round."

"Here's one that looks interesting: a guy who claims that he comes with about $200,000 in billable client work."

"No, too risky. Clients are fickle. With our luck we'll hire the guy, he'll turn out to be a dolt and the client will leave on top of it."

"Herb, the client is his father."

"Oh that's different; I'll put him down for our No. 6 slot."

"Here's somebody who looks good: She has a top record from a good law school and has had two years of solid litigation experience at a New York law firm. She appears to have all of the moves. The scouting report says, 'Flips off answers to interrogatories quickly, articulate on her feet, and a dynamic citechecker.' "

"I noticed her about a week ago. She looked interesting, so I contacted her agent."

"Her agent? She has an agent?"

"Of course, most of your top associates are hiring agents."

"Who are they getting to act as their agents?"

"Some of them are getting football and basketball agents, others are using former headhunters who have been put out of business by our new lateral draft system. You can always tell the agent's background from his cover letter."

"How?"

"Well, listen to these and see:

> "You give my boy, Eddie, a shot and he's going to score for you. Let's just say you're in a tight spot, fourth and goal, down to your final argument. Just hand old Eddie the litigation ball and he'll punch it over."

> "Enclosed herewith are approximately thirty-seven photocopies of resumes of clients of mine, each of whom has outstanding credentials and would fit especially well into your particular firm, corporation or governmental entity. If you want 'em, my cut is 30 percent."

"Yeah, I see what you mean, Herb. But what kind of negotiations do you get into with these agents?"

"Well, this lady from the Chicago firm, her agent wanted a $5,000 signing bonus and a 3-year, no-cut contract. She also wanted a guarantee that all her work would be in litigation and that she would be billed no lower than second on any briefs on which she worked."

"Sounds like she's trying to drive a pretty tough bargain."

"That's nothing compared to what some of them want, Alphonse—guaranteed partnerships, minimum guaranteed income and a corner office with a view."

"Well, what are the other firms doing about these demands?"

"Most are granting them. . . . Hey, Alphonse, where the hell are you going?"

"I'm going to trade our draft choices this year for six or eight choices in 1998."

"Why in the world would you do that?"

"I'm going to start to make a market in 'em."

"Make a market?"

"Why not? Beats the hell out of soybeans—associate futures. I'm bullish."

ASSOCIATES

Introduction

The large number of new associates who fluxed into our firm brought along their own problems. We had to train them, try to keep them happy and healthy, evaluate them and fire them.

Our difficulty in dealing with some of these issues was attributable in part to the inflated expectations that we pumped into these kids during the recruitment process. And, in part, to our incompetence in handling the issues.

Reflecting on the plight of the associate in a firm such as mine, I find that I'm able to muster more empathy than I would have thought. It's not easy to go through life wildly successful, be wined and dined by prestigious employers, offered outrageous salaries and then find that you're really at the bottom of the heap, after all.

But I can't wax too sympathetic; there are a hell of a lot worse sentences than a term at Fairweather, Winters & Sommers.

Time Flies

Set forth below is a transcription of the main speech at the
28th Annual Stanley J. Fairweather Testimonial Dinner,
given for new associates of Fairweather, Winters & Sommers
at the conclusion of their orientation period, to help them
acclimate to the practice. The principal speaker at the dinner
was Stanley J. Fairweather.

Ladies and Gentlemen:

Thank you for that generous, but entirely accurate,
introduction. It is indeed an honor for me to have been
chosen for the 28th consecutive year to deliver this prestigious address. For my topic tonight I have chosen a subject that is the very guts of the practice of law—time
sheets.

While it is not, strictly speaking, essential to understand the theory of relativity in order to fill out time
sheets, it certainly doesn't hurt to have a grasp of the
rudiments. Most honest physicists will acknowledge that
relativity can be boiled down to two fundamental principles—there is no such thing as absolute time, and
quarter-hour segments are as good as any other unit.

The implications of these two principles to time
sheets and to the philosophy of time are apparent upon a
moment's reflection. To time sheets, the absence of absolute time and the acceptability of quarter-hour segments
make it perfectly kosher to bill a quarter hour for a
quickie telephone call. To the philosophy of time, these
principles make the much-heralded accuracy of the quartz
watch of dubious import.

For you young associates, time sheets can be among
the most unpleasant tasks you must face—next to the long
hours that you will be required to put in, the lack of
appreciation expressed for those long hours, dealing with

stupid or overly demanding clients, and dealing with stupid or overly demanding partners. Though not taught in either law school or the bar review course, the art of keeping time sheets separates the merely competent lawyer from the real giant of the profession. So, listen up.

Inevitably, ethics enters into the billing process, however slightly. At least to this extent, though: DON'T GET YOUR HAND CAUGHT IN THE COOKIE JAR.

This is good advice, for sure. True enough, it has precious little to do with billing, but good advice is scarce enough that one should not look a gift horse in the mouth—unless, naturally, you happen to be an equine-dontist and, even then, it's best to leave it to your dental hygienist who, almost invariably, will suggest flossing after each billing.

For those looking to develop a bibliography on the subject, the well-known monograph "On Billing," written by an absent-minded philosopher who neglected to sign the tract, is a "must-read." And if you dabble in Spanish, "La Cuenta, Por Favor" is instructive and provides additional valuable advice on tipping in Mexican restaurants.

Within the bounds of ethics, as aforesaid, and ever mindful of ethical constrictions, there are more than eight acceptable ways of keeping time records.

Leave us turn first to **the anal compulsive record keeper.** This person notes every fifteen minutes what he has done during the preceding quarter hour, and records every detail. A typical fifteen-minute segment will read something like this: "Pulled file out of bottom-right credenza drawer, sustained minor paper cut pulling folder out of tightly-packed file, applied tourniquet and round flesh-colored band-aid, checked firm medical policy for paper-cut coverage, dictated memo to insurance committee re same, and dispatched my secretary to fetch me some coffee (one cream, two sugars), opened folder and recorded time."

The rough justice time keeper hasn't the self-discipline to record his time accurately, and figures it will

all balance out in the long run, anyway. His thought processes go something like the following: "Got in 'bout 8:30 A.M. and left 'round 6:45 P.M.—that's 10 1/4 hours. Took about 1 3/4 hours for lunch, that leaves 8 1/2; two coffee breaks totalin' roughly 3/4 hour, leaves 7 3/4; half hour talking to friends on the phone and another 1/2 hour at the health club—down to 6 3/4 hours. Worked on three matters—6 3/4 divided by 3 is roughly 2 1/4 hours for each matter."

Attorneys with a strong commitment to social justice, but not to personal morality, may opt for **the social justice technique**, which requires doubling the time charged to clients who are "socially culpable," i.e., polluters, bribers, etc., and halving the time of clients who are do-gooders. The social justice technique is a refinement of **the deep-pocket billing theory** (sock it to the largest client) used by attorneys without a commitment to either social justice or personal morality.

The I'll-bill-what-I'm-worth system is the favorite of attorneys with robust egos. For such a one, five minutes on the telephone inflicting his expertise on a client is easily worth six hours of the time of any mortal lawyer, and is billed accordingly. This means of charging permits the biller to develop a flashy golf game, since he can tee off at 10 A.M., having already billed fourteen hours. He trims his golf score by stroke-counting as creatively as he bills.

Nor should we forget the ever-popular **time-padder phylum**, of which one genus is *Determinata avancata*. An attorney belonging to this genus figures out in advance the number of hours he wants to bill for the day and distributes it willy-nilly among clients he's worked for in the recent past. Another time-padder genus is **the double-billed lawyer.** Having an identical problem for two clients, this genus spends an hour on it and bills the hour to each of two clients.

Some former psych majors become **BM (behavior modification) billers**, gauging the time they charge a client on how pleasant it is to deal with that client. Thus, an obnoxious and demanding client gets socked a quarter of an hour for asking the time of day, while a congenial type escapes with hours of free legal advice. This technique might be sensible if it resulted in the obnoxious client becoming less obnoxious. It doesn't—it only results in his complaining about the amount of his bill.

Of course, I do not mean by the above to impugn the integrity of all those called to the bar—only most. There are those who wrestle honestly with the nitty-gritty moral problems involved in billing. Of these, none is knottier than the question of whether one should bill for bathroom time. Clearly the answer to this is not a simple "yes" or "no." For many lawyers, bathroom time is their most productive and profound thinking time. For such an attorney, the question may well evolve to "Should I bill double for this time?" For another, it may not in fact be productive time, but billing may be justified on any of three rationales:

❖ Most of the person's other time is not produc-·tive either, so why discriminate against bathroom time?

❖ Even if it was not productive time, thinking about the client's matter deprived the attorney of a potentially pleasurable experience and, therefore, jolly well ought to be billed.

❖ The bathroom time was necessary to make the subsequent time productive.

Travel time also is pregnant with acute moral problems. Is it fair to penalize a client because a mode of transport is unavailable? For example, if no flights are available from Chicago to New York, is it right to sock the client for the full time required to travel the distance by rickshaw? Or conversely, just because a plane is available, why shouldn't the client, particularly if it is a wholly-owned subsidiary in the Orient, be billed for the full rickshaw time?

Of course, it is impossible to deal with all of the complexities of time sheets in so short a speech, even one as well thought out as this one. You'll have to learn from your mistakes. Just don't make too many. I've got to toddle off now, lest I aggravate my own problem of how to bill for the time spent writing and delivering this speech.

In closing, I'd like to welcome you all to my firm. Remember, if you ever have a problem, my door is always open. Unfortunately, I'm rarely in. Though I may not get to know you by name, I wish you all well, because, when you do well, I do very well indeed.

Turn About Is Fair Play

Before its dissolution owing to the morale problems it was causing, the Fairweather Winters & Sommers Committee on Associate Morale wrestled regularly with the problem of how to make associates happy. A recent search through the committee archives unearthed a tape from which the following transcript of a Morale Committee meeting was produced.

"What seems to be the problem with them this time?"

"Well, it can't be salary. We just gave them all an across-the-board $10,000 bonus and a 25 percent salary increase."

"But that was well over a month ago. Maybe they're expecting something this month again."

"No, I have it on good authority that money isn't it."

"Well, are they complaining about the amount of work?"

"No, I think we took care of that one when we instituted the policy that any associate could turn down any assignment that was tendered to him, if he felt pushed."

"Well, there used to be a problem of their feeling that their work was not being fully appreciated; have we cleared that one up?"

"Yes, I think so. We haven't had many complaints since we went to the 'thank-you-note' policy, using the firm form thank-you-note to associates."

"I don't remember our approving a form thank-you."

"Here, I've got a copy, let me read it to you:

> Dear _____,
>
> Thank you so much for the lovely job that you did on your recent memo. It was so sweet of you to do it for us. I hope that you found the topic interesting enough and that having to put your conclusions in writing wasn't too burdensome or inconvenient.
>
> I just loved reading the memo, so much so that I showed a copy to my spouse, who commented on what a gift you had for working with words (with which we lawyers so often find ourselves working). Were it not for the low-grade trash that passes as cinematic art these days, I would suggest that you seriously consider making the memo into a movie.
>
> Thanks again. Keep up the good work. Hope to see you around the office real soon.
>
> Love and kisses. . .

"And don't forget, we wanted to make sure they felt that the clients loved them, too. So we took to sending them flowers in the clients' names, with a little card that said, 'Thanks for the bang-up job.' "

"Yes, that was a nice touch."

"Well, if they're not underpaid, overworked or under-appreciated, then what do you suppose it is that's bugging the poor dears this time?"

"I wondered that, too, so I found a few of them playing chinese checkers in the coffee room and decided to talk to them about it."

"Well, what did you learn?"

"Not much."

"Figures. They must have told you something, though."

"Well, I took some notes. Let me look. Yes, here are my notes from my talk with John Lewis. He said, 'I don't know exactly what it is, but something just doesn't seem right.' "

"Well, that's helpful. At least we know that the problem is 'something.' We're not just tilting at windmills."

"Here's what Sally Frank-Waller had to say: 'It just doesn't seem like we're, well, part of it, you know, one of you. It's like you're running it up there and we're down here and we're not on the same level and all, you know.'"

"Articulate little devils, aren't they? Sally must have been a moot court champ."

"I hate to admit this, but I think I understand. They seem to be saying they don't feel part of the firm, that they don't have any control over how the place is run."

"Maybe you're right, but what do we do about it? We can't just turn the place over to them."

"Well, this may be a wild idea, but maybe we can turn it over to them, for awhile. I remember, as a lad, going to summer camp. . ."

"So do I! Camp Indianola. I remember those canoe trips and the baseball games and tennis and sailing and all. Those sure were fun times."

"Anyway, there used to be one day at camp when the campers became the counselors and ran the camp. We called it Camper-Counselor Day. Maybe what we need at the firm is an Associate-Partner Day in which all of the associates become partners and run the firm for a day. They could take over our big offices, use our secretaries, talk on speaker phones, go to the club for lunch—just like the big lawyers do. They'd love it."

"That sounds like a great idea. Let *them* deal with clients complaining about bills, decide which new word processors to order and figure out how to tell an associate he'd better start looking for another job. That way they can see the problems that we have, that not everything is roses once you become a partner."

"But how will we decide which associate becomes which partner? They'll all want to be Stanley Fairweather, just like we do."

"That's their problem. Let them figure it out as part of being partners."

So, at the suggestion of the Morale Committee the firm instituted an Associate-Partner Day. For a few hours, associates had a ball in their fancy offices, dictating letters and asking their secretaries to hold their calls. But by about three in the afternoon, the associates began to realize how tough it was to be a partner, and they stopped complaining about being associates.

But Associate-Partner Day created another problem, one that the Morale Committee had not reckoned with. When associates learned how unrosy it was to be a partner, they began to leave the firm in droves. This led eventually to the formation of the Fairweather, Winters & Sommers Committee on Associate Retention and Evaluation, CARE. But that's another story.

Outplacement for Profit

The ad hoc Committee on Associate Retention and Evaluation (CARE) convened the other day when five members of the committee happened to run into one another in the hall and ducked into a nearby conference room. This procedure was in accordance with firm regulations that require ad hoc committees to meet on an ad hoc basis, without reserving a conference room and without charging the firm coffers for lunch.

Stephen Falderall, chair of the ad hoc committee, started by saying, "We've got to do something about the alarming rate at which our young associates are leaving the firm. In the last six months we've lost eight attorneys, and the Lateral Hiring Committee has only managed to replace six of them. At that rate, in thirty years we will have zero attorneys, which will make it rather difficult to service some of our larger clients."

"Yes," added Geodfrey Bleschieu, "it's getting depressing I hate that offensive moment of silence associates have instituted for their departed brethren, in which they all stop whatever it is they are doing at 10:30 each morning and stand with their heads bowed, facing east."

Emanuel Candoo said that he thought it was important that the committee analyze the problem, because things weren't always what they seemed to be. Encouraged by the Chair to spell out his thoughts, since the committee had already obtained the necessary exemption from the general "no analysis" rule that applied to FWS committees, Emanuel said, "It may just be that since the firm is so much larger than it used to be when it was smaller, people are just noticing more that people are leaving. Perhaps, the actual percentage of attorneys leaving is no greater than it was in the past."

Lydia Dos said that the figures showed that the percentage of associates leaving the firm had, in fact, skyrocketed. "Any more bright ideas, Emanuel?" she asked in a tone that some might interpret as hostile or condescending, but not Emanuel.

Hector Morgan thought that the trouble might lie with the salary structure. "We've got to stop paying them what they're worth. It puts us too far below all of the other firms in the area, which are paying their young lawyers the 'going rate.' Maybe if we start paying them the going rate, they'll stop going."

But Lydia pointed out that the firm had already upped associate salaries, so that could not be the problem.

"We've got to give them an incentive to stick around," said Hector. "Like maybe we should take the time-honored Chicago approach: hire some guys to break their kneecaps if they don't stay."

Falderall thought that while Morgan's kneecap proposal had a certain gut-level appeal, it presented potential public relation problems. "It seems to me," said Falderall, "that we are losing an awful lot of people to our competitors and that many of the people we are losing are being picked off by headhunters. We all know how those headhunters work. They just go through the phone book and call up our lawyers. If we instituted the simple procedure of screening phone calls for our young associates (we could tell them we were doing it to ease their work load), we might head off more losses."

Lydia thought that, aside from the fact that Falderall's idea was illegal, unethical, nonsensical and wouldn't work, there was no compelling reason not to implement it pronto.

"Y'know, I was just thinking," Geodfrey interrupted with words that raised an inevitable groan among committee members. "Our problem is associate retention, right? It's associates who treat this place as a sort of revolving door. If we didn't have associates, we wouldn't have an associate retention problem. Now the way I see it, there are two ways we can go with this thing. First, we could make all of these people partners. Partners seem never to leave us. They don't even seem to die. Becoming a partner at our firm seems to be the way to immortality.

"But if you don't like that idea, and I can see that it could present certain problems if we made partners out of kids right out of law school, then we could just call them something else. I think the name associate sounds too important. It makes them think they're hot stuff and should be treated special. Why not call them something a little more like what they are? Say, pledges or apprentices?"

"I've got it," Emanuel said. "We've been thinking of this in the wrong way. All of us have been suggesting ways of solving this supposed problem that we have. I believe that we should stop thinking of it as a problem and begin to think of it as an opportunity.

"For one thing, headhunters around the country are making millions of bucks a year on lawyers that we and others like us have trained. They take our assets, or at least assets that we have enhanced greatly, and sell them off to others. Why not do that ourselves?

"As we hire new attorneys, we could require them to sign an agreement giving to us, in exchange for the invaluable training that we give to them and the outrageous salaries that we pay to them for the privilege of providing them this training, the exclusive right to place them in their next job. We might even agree to guarantee that we will place them. Hell, we can always stick them with some large client, where they'll soon be making four times what we make and, in no time, will become our bosses.

"While that may cause some hiring problems, our public relations people ought to be able to package it so that it's a definite plus. You know: 'We care. We look after all of our people. Even the few who do not stay at FWS are guaranteed a job by our new outplacement department.'

"And all of this is only a few short steps from where I can see us a few short years down the road. The Cubs and Bears trade their players. Why shouldn't the FWS team be in a position to trade its associates? After all, it's impossible to predict your needs from year to year. Clients' needs change and, besides, clients come and go. Why should we be in the position of having hired thirteen crackerjack antitrust lawyers to handle a couple of big cases, only to see those cases settled all at once, leaving us with three big new real estate clients and thirteen useless FTC types? If we could swap them, we might just find a firm in the reverse position. Sure, the firm might be in Fairbanks, Alaska, but that's life in the big city. If we couldn't find a match, we might still be able to unload the trustbusters in return for some future law student draft choices.

"And now, if you'll excuse me, I have an important phone call to make. I've got to call the president of the Topps bubble gum and card company to tell him about a great new idea—associate trading cards, six to a package, with a piece of bubble gum in every pack."

The Feline Perk

Law firms seeking to distinguish themselves from the pack turned, years ago, to offering new and inventive perquisites to lure law students into their lairs. Simply offering more money—besides being crass—did not work. When a few firms upped their starting salary, others upped theirs. This cycle got expensive, since a jump at the bottom of the scale generally meant increases up the line. So law firms turned to perks to snare new associates.

Early attempts were mundane, and wide of the mark. Paying moving expenses, popping for bar review and bar exam fees, and flying spouses in for interview trips soon became expected, passé as perks. And as firms changed the focus from hiring to retaining their associates, perks largely disappeared in recruiting.

But good old American enterprise is responding to the challenge of how to retain associates. And perks are making a comeback. FWS CARE Chair, Stephen Falderall, spoke recently to Mr. E. Allen Rewardsworthy, who left his law practice to head a new firm, Perquisearch (un)Ltd. What follows is a transcript of that discussion:

Q. Mr. Rewardsworthy. . .

A. Yes.

Q. Can you tell me what led you to form Perquisearch (un)Ltd.?

A. Yes.

Q. Well, what led you to form Perquisearch (un)Ltd.?

A. Well, that's a tough question.

Q. Could you answer it?

A. Yes.

Q. Well, what did lead you to form Perquisearch (un)Ltd.?

A. Really, Q., it was a combination of factors. First of all, I perceived a need. Second of all, it seemed that I could perform a service both to the firm that was seeking to retain its associates and to the associates who were seeking to be retained by the firm. Third of all, it seemed an opportunity to make, shall we say, a dutyload of money. Fourth of all, nobody else was doing it. Fifth of all, my law partnership was not doing too well. Sixth of all, my marriage was on the rocks.

Q. May I interrupt you?

A. Yes, but later. Seventh of all, nothing ventured, nothing. . .

Q. Really, Rewardsworthy, I don't have the whole day. Can you give me any hint as to what sorts of perks we may see in the '90s?

A. Of course and, if I may be forgiven the presumption of anticipating your next query, I foresee a move to the more offbeat perk, something not connected with law practice.

Q. I suspect, if I asked, the answer to the question of whether you could give us an example of a perk for the '90s would be "yes."

A. Affirmative.

Q. Well, then?

A. A cat.

Q. You are proposing that law firms give associates a cat as a perk instead of, say, a larger bonus?

A. Yup. Everybody gives money. And associates are overpaid, even without a bonus. They don't need more money.

Q. But why do they need a cat?

A. Glad you asked. New associates at major law firms are worked real hard. They are abused. They are the lowest of the low. What they need is something alive that they can kick around, and what better than a cat?

Q. Assuming that a guardian angel from the SPCA has not yet struck you dead for that remark, why a cat? Why not, for example, a person's best friend—the dog?

A. Young associates are worked too hard to care for a canine. Dogs have to be walked periodically or else they'll mess up your apartment, condominium or suburban home. A kitty, on the other hand, will use a cozy box of kitty litter. Though months of non-attention may render the cat neurotic, months of late nights and weekends at the firm will render the associate a comrade in arms.

Q. Do you find law firms receptive to the services of Perquisearch (un)Ltd.?

A. So far, I've sold 2,840 cats to 32 firms, each of which thinks that I've come up with a unique idea for their firm.

Q. Do you have any other ideas for perks, and can you tell us about them?

A. On the one hand, yes. On the other hand, no.

Q. How do you approach law firms about signing on as clients of Perquisearch (un)Ltd.?

A. Generally, I approach a senior partner in the firm and offer that partner a free sample of any perk that the firm opts for. This technique was extremely successful in our promotion of a "significant other" as a perk.

Q. Do you see Perquisearch (un)Ltd. as a firm that can go on forever, merely thinking of new and more innovative perks?

A. No, Q., frankly I don't. What I see is that a little ways down the road we at Perquisearch (un)Ltd. will have loaded associates' dwellings with cats, gnus, kangaroos, nudibranchs, etc. to the point where their homes will be almost as much of a zoo as their law firms. At that point, Perquisearch (un)Ltd. will come up with the ultimate perk, or antiperk. It will offer associates a firm free of clothing allowances, signing bonuses, fancy recruiting dinners and the like, a place where an associate can practice an interesting brand of law, be paid a decent wage and be offered security, training and, ultimately, the prospect of partnership. Then Perquisearch (un)Ltd. will die or wither away. I'll join that firm, because that's why I thought I went to law school in the first place.

Q. Thank you.

A. Don't mention it.

Undue Process

Once upon a time at Fairweather, Winters & Sommers, associates took what was given to them and were glad of it. But no more.

Now, at the time of annual salary increases in June, and again at bonus time in December, associates are given extensive evaluations of their work, along with the news about their raise or bonus. The procedure used in this evaluation has been refined from time to time as the need arises. Here is the latest version:

To: **All Partners**
From: **Committee on Associate Retention and Evaluation (CARE)**
Re: **New Associate Evaluation Procedures**

This memo is in response to certain criticisms of our prior evaluation procedure received from the Associate Grievance Committee. It supersedes in its entirety the memo of last December, which superseded the memo of last July in its entirety, which superceded the memo of the previous December in its entirety, all in response to certain criticisms of the then existing evaluation system as graciously pointed out to CARE by the then incumbent Associate Grievance Committee. As always, CARE is extremely grateful to all of the associates who have devoted so many of their otherwise billable hours to helping us solve these difficult problems. Their selfless devotion to a just resolution of these problems is an inspiration to us all.

Here, then, are the revised rules:

Each April 15 and October 15, the partnership shall announce to the associates its intention to conduct an evaluation of associates' performance. Notice shall be given to each associate via office mail, return receipt requested.

Each associate shall have two weeks from receipt of the notice to decide whether he or she wishes to participate in the evaluation. In the event that an associate elects not to participate in the evaluation, then such associate shall be awarded a salary increase or bonus, as the case may be, equal to the greater of (a) the associate's last such increase or bonus, adjusted upward for any increase in the cost of living, or (b) the average salary increase or bonus awarded to those associates in the abstaining associate's class.

If an associate elects to participate in the evaluation, he or she may designate three partners to be disqualified from participating in the associate's evaluation. These shall be regarded as peremptory disqualifications. In addition, the associate shall be entitled to disqualify any other partner for good cause shown. Because of the fear of reprisals, if an associate claims to have good cause to disqualify a partner from participating in an evaluation, he shall present his case to an impartial tribunal of three associates chosen by the associate being evaluated and meeting *in camera*.

If an electing associate succeeds in disqualifying all partners by reason of his peremptory challenges and his challenges for cause, then the associate shall be entitled to make his own determination as to the amount of the salary increase or bonus to be awarded to him.

All evaluations tendered by non-disqualified partners shall be signed, sworn to and submitted in triplicate. When all evaluations have been received, one copy of the evaluation shall be submitted to the associate, one to counsel for the associate and one to CARE. All expenses of counsel for the associate during these proceedings shall be borne solely by the partnership.

If the associate disagrees strongly with the evaluations submitted, he may request that all or a portion of the evaluations be done over again. In such event, the offending partner shall redo the offensive evaluation and shall use his or her best efforts to do a better job this time.

Each evaluating partner shall, if requested to do so, submit for questioning under oath by the associate and his counsel. Prior to this questioning, the associate may submit interrogatories or requests for production of documents to the evaluating partner.

After testimony from the partner, the associate may call rebuttal witnesses or may take the stand in his own defense. The associate shall also have the right to call witnesses to testify to the character of the associate or to disparage or heap scorn upon the evaluating partner.

When all testimony has been received, CARE shall meet to consider the evaluation of the associate. The associate shall have the right to attend and be represented by counsel at all CARE meetings.

In conducting its evaluations, CARE shall resolve all disputes in favor of the associate. Testimony given by the associate in his own behalf shall be presumptively true, unless rebutted by clear and convincing evidence given by at least three partners. Within two weeks of hearing the last of the testimony, CARE shall render a written decision.

Any associate aggrieved by a decision of CARE shall have the right to appeal the decision to the Executive Committee, sitting *en banc*. A decision of CARE shall be reversed by the Executive Committee if the associate makes a fairly decent case that something CARE did was incorrect, unfair or otherwise contrary to the best interests of the associate.

If the associate fails to convince the Executive Committee to change a decision of CARE, then the associate may appeal to Stanley J. Fairweather, who may do anything he wants.

These new rules will go into effect immediately. If the Associate Grievance Committee is dissatisfied with any aspect of the new rules as they actually operate, they have promised to let us know forthwith.

If these rules seem overly generous to you, it is probably because of a deficiency in your legal education relative to the evolution of the concept of procedural due process. CARE has been assured that the proposed new rules go no further than any self-respecting court of justice would require in any event. We are confident in relying on this advice, since it is being given to us by some of the top law students of the last decade. We must remember that these kids hold the key to the future success of this firm. If we take unfair advantage of these poor little defenseless darlings, we will only be hurting ourselves in the long run. We adopt these rules in the hope that if we are good to the associates now, they will be good to us later when we are too old to support ourselves in the manner to which we have become accustomed.

You've Gone About As Far As You Can Go, Lex

"May there be sufficient salt in your life that your thirst for knowledge be never quenched" is the loose translation of the famous Armenian proverb that is painted freehand above the ivy-laden door of the conference room that serves as the FWS continuing legal education center.

FWS takes its Continuing Legal Advancement Program (CLAP) seriously. Born of an unfortunate malpractice action filed against FWS from federal prison by a vindictive client who was advised in 1943 that he need not pay his income tax because the tax code was clearly unconstitutional, CLAP is administered by a committee of six, headed by Dean Fairweather.

Not all associates are admitted to CLAP (partners are exempt from CLAP, since you don't get to be a partner unless you know the law). Participation is gained through competitive examination. In fact, some enterprising partners have parlayed CLAP into a lucrative side business, running cram courses for associates who are clammering to do well on their CLAP boards (or, as one wag put it, on their wainscoting). While some have argued that the course slogan, "After a few nights with us, you'll score well and get the CLAP," is in poor taste, few can argue with the course's success record.

Generous gifts from the Fairweather Foundation, to which every FWS partner voluntarily contributes 2.3 percent of his gross income, have permitted CLAP to establish seven endowed chairs and to hire a faculty second to none. The stature of the current faculty continues a tradition that has evolved from former greats, such as Learned Hand, whose tenure on the faculty gave rise to one of the most misunderstood quotations of all time.

It seems that one day, while Learny was lecturing, two FWS partners were standing outside the conference room door and one asked the other, "What's that noise?" The response of the other was the now famous remark, "That's the sound of one Hand, CLAPing."

The Fairweather Foundation scholarship fund has built up a considerable balance in recent years, since scholarships are doled out on the basis of need. Dean Fairweather has taken the position that, at the salary levels currently paid to FWS associates, none of them qualifies as needy.

FWS associates who excel in the CLAP program are placed on "Stan's List" and are eligible to work on the *Fairweather Journal of Continuing Legal Education*. The editor-in-chief of the journal is traditionally selected to present the Dean with a gift at the annual Stanley J. Fairweather Testimonial Dinner. The top five percent annually are elected to membership in the firm honor society, Phi Beta Clappa.

CLAP has followed the lead of other continuing legal education programs by arranging exotic tax-deductible trips, on which educational programs are offered. Last year's raft trip down the Omo River in Ethiopia, on which ERISA was discussed, *ad nauseam*, may be counted a huge success but for the loss by poison dart of three associates. The uncordial natives seemed more concerned with an invasion of vested rafters than with the vesting of their pension benefits. A protest to Emperor Haile Selassie fell on deaf ears, the emperor having died a decade or two earlier.

This year's trip to Switzerland will concentrate on the question of whether a yodel can be sent return receipt requested and, if so, why?

By nature a continuing program, designed to give participants a sense of accomplishment, CLAP holds an annual graduation ceremony at which Dean Fairweather is traditionally the commencement speaker and an honorary degree recipient. Last year's speech was thought by many, himself included, to be one of his finest efforts. Excerpts are therefore set forth below:

"Let me first thank the Commencement Ceremony Speaker's Committee for selecting me once again to be the principal speaker. The honor I feel today is not diminished a whit by the fact that this marks the 27th consecutive year that I have delivered this address.

"This is indeed a great day. As I marched down the aisle to 'Pomp and Circumstance' a tear welled in my eye and a lump grew in my throat. And I intend to see my ENT-man about both of these problems.

"But more to the point, I would like to address you today on what I see as the future of continuing legal education in this country, in general and, in this firm, in particular.

"First within the firm, I see it continuing exactly as it is now, because I'm running the show and I am well pleased with the job that I have been doing. While some have sniped at this or that aspect of the program, most have had the good sense to keep their mouths shut.

"Nationally, I see competing considerations warring over the next several years. On the one hand, there is the interest of the bar and the public in having lawyers who are educated on the current state of the law, rather than on its state at the time of their graduation from law school. In this regard, there can be little doubt that one who graduated from law school after adoption of the Uniform Commercial Code is likely to have a richer appreciation of the factors governing certain commercial transactions today than a lawyer weaned on the Sales Act.

"On the other hand, it must be recognized that continuing legal education does not come cheaply, and that any attempt to pass these costs along to consumers of legal services may have the effect of helping further to price legal services out of the marketplace. Thus the choice may well boil down to whether it is better to have affordable lawyers who know what the law used to be or unaffordable lawyers who know what the law is.

"Of course, there is another alternative—to eliminate the need for continuing legal education by stopping the evolution of the law. We should ask ourselves whether, after hundreds of years of evolution, the law hasn't really come far enough. Sure, we could always graft on a few more nuances. But is it really worth destroying the economic footings upon which the law and therefore our society are built?

"Some will argue that society is changing and that the law must change with it. But that has it backwards. The law, rather than reacting to change, has been the primary instrument of social change. Therefore, by stopping the evolution of the law, we will stop the need for the evolution of the law as well.

"So I say to you graduates today, as you take this significant step in your lives, 'Enough is enough.' We don't need more evolution of the law. That evolution is ripping apart the very fabric of our society. And not even at a seam.

"What we need is a freeze on changes in the law, both

statutory and common. Not necessarily a permanent freeze; say a century, for starters."

The extent of the favorable reaction to Dean Fairweather's speech may perhaps best be gauged by the volume of applause, which at one point reached such a crescendo that the Dean was forced to greet the audience with index fingers stuck in both his ears. Fortunately, an associate was present on either side of the Dean so that he could do this while leaving both his hands free to wave in acknowledgment of the throng's enthusiasm.

With the aid of several associates, Dean Fairweather's commencement speech was recast, footnoted elaborately and published in scholarly journals under titles ranging from "Changes in the Law: A Cost-Benefit Analysis" to "Law and Social Change: Which Came First, the Chicken or the Lex." These articles have somehow found their way onto the required reading list for next year's CLAP syllabus. And FWS has been fortunate to land as its guest lecturer on the topic "Is Legal Evolution Worth Monkeying Around With?" the progenitor of the debate on that subject, Stanley J. Fairweather.

Health Makes Wealth

Health scarcely can be said to be irrelevant to the practice of law. After all, a clean body does make for a clean mind and cleanliness is adjacent to godliness. This is not to suggest, of course, that one must break up an important conference call to do a brace of push-ups. And there are unquestionably some excellent fat lawyers, mainly in real estate. Nonetheless, it is tough to maintain the posture of a no-nonsense litigator from an oxygen tent.

Formed primarily to address associate concerns about the sagging quality of life at the firm (but supported by the pronouncement of the firm's public relations agency, Keepum Fortha Public, that "health sells"), the Fairweather, Winters & Sommers Committee on Health in Practice (CHIP) is charged with responsibilities ranging from "assuring a tidy loo" to "developing associate bodies." Under the stewardship of Vance "Rip" Winkle III, the committee has tackled its tasks with gusto and ingenuity, as the following transcript of the committee report, tendered at the last partnership meeting, will attest:

A healthy good evening to you all. We on CHIP are right proud of our first year of operation and gung ho to report to you tonight.

First off, we hope you enjoyed your dinner. Some of you may have noticed that instead of the traditional beef Wellington, with thousands of calories and God-knows-what in that poor dead cow, we substituted a plate of natural alfalfa. We trust that you all will prefer the tart apple for dessert to our normal *tarte tatin*. And starting tomorrow, our new emphasis on healthier foods will pump its way into the firm vending machine. Granola and raisins will replace Baby Ruths and Butterfingers; V-8 will be stocked in lieu of good old Mountain Dew.

No doubt many of you have spotted the ALL ATTORNEYS MUST WASH BOTH OF THEIR HANDS BEFORE RETURNING TO WORK placards we've posted in the bathrooms around the firm. It is our impression that this policy has gained gradual acceptance. Complaints of "overkill" which we were receiving early-on from associates who claimed they "wiped real good and carefully," have virtually disappeared, of late. We recognize, of course, that there is another plausible explanation for the drop-off in these complaints, but we prefer to assume that compliance is now widespread.

Gratefully, we are now at last beyond the question raised by one of our associates as to whether the committee had overstepped its bounds in requiring hand washing. This issue was laid to rest by the opinion we obtained from the local bar association ethics committee, which held that the requirement that an attorney avoid "even the appearance of impropriety" fully justified our regulation.

Progress is being made, we are pleased to report, on the firm drinking problem. The initial resistance to the requirement of taking a breathalizer test upon return from lunch has now dissipated substantially. Fully two-thirds of our lawyers now cheerfully take, and almost one half pass, these tests daily. And the formation of a firm AA Chapter in Conference 72 North has turned out to be a master stroke, giving comfort to the 76 lawyers who attend regularly, knowing they are not alone.

With the drinking problem in hand, the committee tends to devote more of its attention to ferreting out the drug-pushing associates, hopefully before they corrupt yet more of our senior partners. We do not regard it as either cute or consonant with our image as a prestigious law firm to have several of our senior partners snorting coke in the bathroom stalls. Even on the purely practical level, this creates obvious problems for people who justifiably would like to use the stalls for other purposes.

Sadly, our anti-smoking campaign has run into stiff resistance. Our placement around the corridors of X rays of the lungs of heavy smokers has provoked protests from the Art Committee, which, unfortunately, have been sustained by our Executive Committee. Accordingly, we have had to resort to more subtle techniques, such as instructing the clean-up staff not to empty ashtrays.

Perhaps our greatest success to date, however, is the general enthusiasm that our associates have shown for our renewed emphasis on FWS sports teams. In this regard, we have high hopes for next year's lawyer-league basketball season, as our Hiring Committee has graciously acceded to employing a 6-foot-11-inch center, Tom Boerwinklesque, who languished unnoticed in the bottom quarter of his class at Harold Carswell University School of Law for the Mediocre until discovered by a CHIP member judging moot court at H.C.U.

By the way, Chairman Winkle has rather taken to being called "Coach" around the firm and trusts that nobody is unduly offended by his tooting twice on his whistle when passing somebody in the hall, rather than saying hello. And to all of those who chipped in for the pinstriped three-piece sweat suit that was given to him, Coach says, "God bless."

While it is true that a certain discomfort level was engendered by the filing of a sex-discrimination suit based upon the unfortunate decision of Coach Winkle to require female paralegals to suit up as cheerleaders, this all seems well behind us now. The committee was genuinely gratified by the recent selection of our firm cheer as the outstanding entry in this year's contest:

> Sue 'em in the courts
> Outsmart 'em at the table
> C'mon you Fairweather Torts
> Show 'em that you're able
> Sock 'em in the briefs
> Give 'em lots of griefs
> Fairweather, Fairweather,
> Rah, Rah, Rah!

Coach Winkle is beginning to feel that the job of coaching all of our sports teams is incompatible with continuing to practice law. Accordingly, we are suggesting that Winkle's title be changed to General Manager and that a fulltime coach be hired for each team. Naturally, the recruiting efforts of the various coaches will have to be coordinated with our Hiring Committee.

A subcommittee of CHIP, seeking to turn the sporting events into profit centers for the firm, is giving preliminary thought, in conjunction with the Space and Finance Committees, to a proposal to build a domed stadium. We are looking into whether industrial revenue bond financing may be available, and have referred to our Ethics Committee the question of whether naming the stadium Stanley J. Fairweather Field would run afoul of ethical constrictions.

Time does not permit us to catalogue all of the exciting proposals our associates have made for next year. Converting our largest conference room to a gymnasium, and cindering a portion of our corridor and designating it a jogging track are but a few of the things on the boards.

CHIP is dedicated to building this firm's reputation across the nation as a healthy place to work. Our aim is to create an image such that when one spies a person carrying an attaché case and looking decidedly in the pink, the first thing to pop to mind will be "Gee, that fellow is looking 'fit as a Fairweather.' "

So Long, It's Been
Good T'Know Ya

To: Partners Conducting Associate Reviews
From: CARE Chair, Stephen Falderall

Hardly anybody likes to be the bearer of bad tidings. The reason for this may be rooted historically in the quaint custom of killing the messenger who bore them. For those who believe that there is a segment of the subconscious in every brain which is occupied exclusively by things historical and which causes people to act in ways that make sense historically—a belief, by the by, that currently is in vogue in parts of Iowa and in suburban Grand Forks, North Dakota . . . I forgot what I was starting to say with this sentence . . . Anyhow, killing the messenger who bore bad tidings went out a long time ago, or Western Union never would have gotten off the ground and there might not be any such thing as a Candy-gram, even today.

If all of this seems a rather long-winded introduction, it may be because the topic that I am slowly but surely trying to blast my way into is not a pleasant one. In fact, it is really a tragic one. It has to do with informing associates in law firms that they aren't making it. In fact, more than having to do with that topic, it is that topic (informing associates in law firms that they aren't making it).

"Why is that such a tragic subject?" some may ask. To answer that question, one must first analyze where "some" is coming from. Is he or she a closet Humanities major challenging whether this is, indeed, tragedy in the sense of, say, Medea? If so, the proper answer probably is something like "no," since last year's statistics show that relatively few associates who were told they weren't making it slew their children. But if "some" is really asking, "What's so sad about all this?", that's a horse of quite a different color (maybe puce).

Why is it sad? For whom is it sad? When is it sad? How is it sad? And where is it sad? All of these are so-called "sad-related questions." But to acknowledge this does not advance the argument a whit. No sir. Nor will it help overly to define "sad" in terms of its opposite, "glad." While it may be true that, for every person who is made sad, another is made glad, this may well not be true or, if true, it may be coincidental. Either way, it makes Newton no less plausible.

Surprisingly, there is precious little literature on the subject of telling associates that they aren't making it. While several state bar journals have published how-to-do-it pieces on the subject, one may scour the index to legal periodicals in vain for a scholarly treatment, unless one regards as qualifying the piece in *Business Lawyer* entitled "Canning the Associate by Proxy: Axing within the Securities Actsies."

This piece suggests that the news be broken to the associate something like this: "The Personnel Committee has solicited proxies on the question of whether you should be employed for another year. Proxies were solicited on behalf of management and were sought only from management, since only management is entitled to vote on the question. It is my unfortunate duty to announce to you that the tellers of the election have now reported: a quorum was present, and you're fired."

There are many different ways to tell an associate that he or she is not making it. The proper method will depend on the personality of the partner charged with lowering the boom, the personality of the boomee and other factors not here relevant. The sensitive hatchet-wielder will also give heed to matters such as place, time, dress and method.

Common choices for place are the partner's office, the

associate's office, the bathroom, the firm's reception area, a conference room, the elevator or a fancy restaurant. Whatever one chooses, it is vital that the associate be made to feel comfy, and not in any way threatened.

Time also can be important. Generally, Christmas time or the associate's birthday are not propitious. About 2:45 P.M., on the other hand, generally is swell.

Dress usually is appropriate, but the type thereof is immaterial. Some axers like to top off their normal garb with a smart-looking hood; others find a hood too impersonal or foreboding.

Methods of letting an associate know that he or she isn't making it may vary as much as places and times—or more so. Generally, notification by post—certified mail, return receipt requested, or otherwise—is inappropriate. And padlocking the associate's office door, while it gets the message across effectively, is a tad too subtle. Our experience is that there just is no substitute for the sheer humanity of a face-to-face axing.

What to say, though, can be easily screwed up and, if left to the whims of partners around here, undoubtedly will be. Aside from the likelihood that most partners, unfamiliar with the associates, will dismiss the wrong associate, a jagged axing may cause bloodshed on surviving associates. The latter, while accepting that some of their brethren and sestren will have to be sacrificed, expect, nonetheless, a nice neat job of it. To minimize the possibility of error, we have developed the following canned canning speech:

"Hi [here insert name of the person you are about to can], it's so very nice to see you. Have a seat. How's the spouse? . . . Good, and the new triplets? . . . Glad to hear it.

"Enjoying yourself at the firm? . . . Good. Lots of interesting work, eh? . . . You say the partners you're working for really seem to have appreciated your work? Glad to hear it. Any problems? . . . None at all, eh? Glad to hear it.

"No, I didn't have anything special in mind, just wanted to say 'how's by you,' as we say . . . er, er. This is quite a demanding place, not for everyone, that's for sure . . . Oh, you find it very *simpatico*, not overly demanding at all? Glad to hear it. No, don't go yet, there is one more thing I wanted to mention in passing. As you may know, I was appointed recently to the firm's Personnel Committee . . . Yes, thank you very much, it is quite an honor. Well, our Personnel Committee just met and we've determined, reluctantly, that certain of our associates are not making it here. . . . Yes, I quite agree that that is rather a shame. Now that's not to say that they are not good lawyers and aren't going to do just fine somewhere else, but this place is not for everyone. Listen, what I'm about to tell you is going to hurt me more than it's going to hurt you, but one of the associates whom we've decided has no future here at all is in this very office . . . Yes, I'll bet you could guess his initials, too. We have always been willing to help associates to find another position and we cer . . . Oh, I'm glad that I saved you the trouble of telling me you had accepted a partnership with another firm, but you really needn't have been dreading telling me . . . You really feel that way about the firm? . . . And about me, too? Well, up yours too, fella! But we do wish you the very best in your legal career."

Partnership Parody

As the snow begins to fly, the Associate Skit Writing Committee for the annual Christmas-Chanukah-New Year's party meets at an undisclosed location to prepare the highlight of the party, the associates' spoof of the partners. The identity of the skit writers is a closely guarded secret owing to a misapprehension held by some of the associates that, in years gone by, retribution was taken against the writers. This charge is steadfastly denied by the partnership, which views as purely circumstantial the fact that, for a four-year period when the identity of the writers was listed on the programs, none of them survived to participate in the following year's party.

Here is a transcript of last year's presentation.

The scene is set in the hallway outside a fancy conference room at FWS, where Randolph Hardass, head of the FWS real estate department and a member of the Executive Committee, passes Vesuvio Voir-Dire, chief of the litigation department and also a member of the EC.

Randolph: Good m'lord, how goes it wi' you?

Vesuvio: Rotten, gentle Randolph. Opposing counsel's motion to dismiss our latest complaint summarily was this day granted.

Randolph: Verily?

Vesuvio: Aye, summarily.

Randolph: But what does this forebode?

Vesuvio: Ill, gentle Randolph. For our client, Consuvio, leader of Consuvio Crossbows International, Inc., will be mightily pissed off when he of the judge's decision doth learn. For Consuvio is not pleasèd e'en when should he be and 'tis certain that when reason he has pissed to be, then so shall he be ten times over. And the matter is worsened still, for I in youthful enthusiasm did hold out to

Consuvio that his damages might thrice their real level be, for the realm hath decreed that 'twill in certain cases be so, though nobody knows wherefore.

Randolph: That soundeth bleak indeed, Vesuvio. Thinkest thou that we might Consuvio as client lose?

Vesuvio: I know not for sure, Randolph, but perchance it may be so. For though Consuvio has long our client been and is by blood related to one of our partners, he has of late foul noises made. He hath demanded of us a billing in detail of all for which we charge him and has asked of our rates, hourly.

Randolph: Not hourly?

Vesuvio: Aye, and sourly, too, he asked it.

Randolph: Things have changed greatly, m'lord, in the matter of clients, thinkest thou not?

Vesuvio *(stepping in front, center stage, to deliver his speech):* Yes, gentle Randolph, of late great changes in clienthood have been wrought. Earlier was a client but once wooed and, when won, forever won. But, alas, 'tis no longer so. Where is clients' constancy that once as a steadfast star didst shine? Where gone the days when a bill, once sent, was paid ere e'en thirty days didst pass? Then was a gentler time, good Randolph, when a round or two of golf would sew tight from year to year relationships, not deserved mayhap, but passed from generation to generation, the seisin held without the breaking of a twig. Then could no loutish other lawyer come 'twixt you and your client, solicit him like whore solicits, steal him and cuckold thee. Such action would the bar association condemn and the whore disbarrèd be. Late, though, law hath business become. E'en business managers have the lofty firms procured, and clients customers become. Oh, Randolph, would 'twere not so. But, forsooth, it is. And I fear it shall ever be so. For the clock cannot be turnèd back and progress, though it ugly be, will not be otherwise, though feign I would pray it so. For lo, what is a client but a normal person with money? And though money the root of evil be, it helpeth the legal bills to pay and thereby our bottom line to enhance. Money falleth not as the gentle rain from heaven nor groweth it on yonder tree, neither doth credit, either. Damnable rogues clients be. Yet, by Jove, we need them still. But soft, Stanley MacFair approacheth.

MacFair: Long-winded Vesuvio, what wert thou discoursing 'pon when thou shouldeth billable work be grinding out?

Vesuvio: Mighty MacFair, think not ill of me, I beseech thee. I was but speaking of that on which lawyers do so frequently soliloquize yet nothing do about—clients.

MacFair: And did you bemoan their lack of constancy?

Vesuvio: I did, good sir.

MacFair: And speak of the times gone by, when a round or two of golf would a relationship sew tight?

Vesuvio: Why, yes sir. That I did.

MacFair: And of lawyer-whores and clocks turnèd not back?

Vesuvio: Why, good sir, you are prescient. That I did. But how came you to know of what I spoke? For you were not here when I spake. Didst thou buggeth me?

MacFair: Simple and long-winded Vesuvio, I knew of what you spake because you do so oft repeat yourself and so little say that a man of brains (and no false modesty halts me from saying that I have those aplenty) by knowing but a little of the time of day and situation can foretell or posttell what you say. So, learning that you had been from out of court blasted by a motion for judgment summary, I required but little thought to know that you would on clients' inconstancy be carping again. Go, get ye thither, back to work and let me not catch thee again farting around. Begone!

Exeunt Vesuvio and Randolph left; MacFair moves front right and speaks.

MacFair: What fools these Executive Committee members be! Oft' think I 'twould better be the Executive Committee to disband so that I, noble Mac-Fair, might rule this fair firm alone again, as once I did. 'Twas a sturdier ship when I its helm alone controlled. And then young upstarts unto me didst come and entreat me, "MacFair, a hand we'd have in steering our ship." So I an Executive Committee in my own image created and have had with them to deal these last many years. And much time and effort have I wasted on these buffoons. As years upon me hang I think sometimes to rid me of this curse. But, hark, the paralegal chorus sings.

Paralegal Chorus:

> Oh we are faira paralegals,
> Pairs of faira legals we,
> We fill forms and have them typèd,
> Typèd for-ems fill and file.
> And while at us 'torneys blither,
> Knowing nither of what they speak,
> We their wretchèd hearts beguile,
> But first we fill the forms, then file,
> File and smile, smile and file,
> Hearts beguile, then smile and file.

MacFair: What ho, dainty paralegals. How go you today?

Felicia (head of the paralegal chorus): Noble MacFair, not well. We have this day heavy hearts for we have learnèd of something that we, as little paralegals, should not know, and since we should not know and yet know we do, we know not what of this knowledge that we know we should impart, and to whom.

MacFair: Dainty Felicia, despaireth not. Tell me, gallant MacFair, noblest Executive Committee member of them all, what it is that buggeth you.

Felicia: But we fear to tell you, noblest of all the Executive Committee and former bar association president. We fear to tell you, because it is knowledge that you affects.

MacFair: Nay, Felicia, fear not knowledge, for knowledge is not to be feared. Rather to be feared is lack of knowledge, which I call ignorance. For if knowledge be feared, then should not ignorance be twice feared, and if ignorance twice feared be, then what of stupidity, huh? So sing forth your knowledge and fear not.

Felicia: Okay, if thou sayest so. Paralegal chorus, on three—a-one and a-two and a-three.

Paralegal Chorus:

> What we fearo,
> Stanley dearo,
> What we fearo it is this:
> Bad Hardass and evil Voir-dire
> Mean to end our firm's long bliss.
> For they plano,
> Dearest Stano,
> You to can-o from our midst.

MacFair: But faith, this I cannot believe. How came you by this information? And take care that you are right. For if you falsely accuse gentle Hardass and simple Voir-dire, who 'til late you spoke I thought the two finest of my Executive Committee members, then it shall not go well for you hence. Get thee gone. Adieu!

Just then, the microphone inexplicably went dead. Stanley J. Fairweather, arising from his seat near the electrical plug, thanked the associates for their clever skit and wished everyone a Merry Christmas, a Happy Chanukah, a joyous New Year and a pleasant good night.

Come Monday, when Francine Hoppens, a recent law school graduate and possessor of a Ph.D. in English Lit. from Farleigh Dickinson, returned to work, she found her desk cleared out, her office locked and this note attached to her door:

> They are but fools who dare
> Cross swords with Lord MacFair.
> *[Exit]*

PARTNERS

Introduction

If the realization that associatehood is not summer camp comes as a surprise to new associates, the revelation that partnership is not nirvana arrives as a thunderbolt to new partners. Having been conditioned to believe that achieving partnership is grasping the golden ring, it comes hard to realize that partnership brings with it more obligations and worries than perquisites.

Even the *Associate Partnership Training Handbook* that we produced—at great expense—failed to ease the difficult transition to partnership. Gradually, though, and sometimes painfully, partners came to realize that some of us are a lot more equal than others, that their slice of the partnership pie may look as if the server thought they were dieting and that nothing, not even partnership, is forever.

Here is how they learned those lessons.

Handbook of Infallibility

Conceived in the heyday of the continuing legal education movement, the Fairweather, Winters & Sommers Committee on Associate Partnership Training is dedicated to the proposition that if you can teach ERISA, you can jolly well teach partnership. APT has been doing its damndest to prove that proposition for three years now, using the most sophisticated techniques developed by Continuing Legal Education buffs to try to measure an FWS associate's APTitude for partnership.

Prospective new partners watch themselves on videotape, observe actual partnership behavior through one-way glass installed outside partners' offices, and spend hours in the FWS sound studios listening to the proper intonations for conversations with receptionists, associates and other partners.

Perhaps the most valuable tool available to would-be partners, though, is the *APT Handbook*. Designed, developed and copyrighted by the Handbook Subcommittee of APT, the work supplements what trainees learn in their hands-on training sessions. While the book must be read from cover to cover to be fully appreciated (and few who pick it up can resist reading it straight through), the introduction sets the tone for what readers can expect throughout. Here it is, in part:

Dedication

To all who would attain partnership: Seek and ye shall find—maybe.

Stanley J. Fairweather
July 1988

Introduction

What is partnership? Partnership is many things to many people. And a few things to a few people.

Partnership can be happiness. It can be wealth. It

can be prestige. It can be a warm, fuzzy feeling. It can be love. Or a new puppy. Or an April shower.

Now that you are on what may be the threshold of partnership, or the precipice of the greatest disappointment of your entire life, you may wonder what you should expect if you are among the chosen. This book is designed to make the transition to partnership easier. It will never be simple; no important growth experience is. (Well, maybe a few, but certainly not the majority.)

It may help if you gain a little historical perspective on partnership—how and why it came to be. The first partnership was Harry Feldman. Harry had a split personality, both of whom chanced to be attorneys. The original firm name was Feldman & Feldman, P.C. Though they inhabited the same body, neither Feldman trusted the other, and both insisted on a written partnership agreement. This mistrust is traditional and has been carried forward in partnerships today, though relatively few partners nowadays inhabit the same body. Most find it tough enough to share office space.

Through therapy, Feldman eventually got better and dissolved the partnership. The healthy Feldman became the proprietor of a video game arcade; the sick Feldman continued to practice as The Law Offices of Harry Feldman.

Over the years, partnerships got bigger, though not necessarily better. And there you have it. (For a more detailed treatment of the evolution of partnerships, see the tract, "From Harry Feldman to Baker & MacKay: A More Detailed Treatment of the Evolution of Partnerships," 47 *Yale L.J.* 483.)

We at FWS have found over the years that, as partnership approaches, lawyers tense up. They are afraid to ask questions about what becoming a partner is all about for fear that those questions will seem silly or presumptuous, or will be misinterpreted. And they're right.

However, it is not healthy emotionally to keep questions about partnership pent up, even if they are silly and presumptuous and liable to be misinterpreted. Better far, we've found, to unpent them. So, to spare you the embarrassment of having to ask these questions, we have collected here some of the most common silly, presumptuous and easily misinterpreted questions, and the answers to them.

Are there objective criteria for admission to partnership?

Of course there are. And as soon as the partners determine what they are, they will be communicated to all associates.

Will I need unanimous approval to become a partner?

Nobody knows. The election is by secret ballot. Stanley J. Fairweather counts.

If I do not make partner the first time that I am considered, is it possible that I may make it another time?

Possible, but not bloody likely.

Will I earn a lot more money as a partner?

Not necessarily. The amount you earn will depend on matters such as how large your partnership share is and how outrageous partnership expenses are.

How large will my partnership percentage be?

Very small indeed.

How outrageous will partnership expenses be?

Quite.

If I will not be earning a lot more money, what are the major benefits of partnership?

People will *think* you are earning a lot more. This will mean that they will expect you not to object to splitting the dinner bill equally, even if you and your spouse have a light snack while the other couple have a full dinner and several drinks apiece. If splitting the bill equally bothers you, consider accountancy.

Will I have a lot more client contact if I become a partner?

Probably. It's hard to avoid it.

Will I be able to attend partnership meetings and, if so, what can I expect to find at them?

Yes, you will be expected to attend. Meetings are devoted primarily to questions of basic partnership policy. For example, the equivalent of $12,000 of billable lawyer time is spent annually deciding whether name tags will be worn at the firm party.

As a partner, I'll have access to more information than I've had as an associate, won't I?

Not really. Nothing important is decided at partnership meetings. Associates generally have better access to information through the rumor mill and do not share the information with younger partners, since associates assume that partners already know. The younger partners are too embarrassed to admit that they don't and therefore remain in the dark, unless clued in by their secretaries.

Is there nothing positive that I can look forward to as a partner?

Of course. Partners get bigger offices and speaker phones. Most find that this makes all those years of hard work well worth it.

Is there nothing else that comes with partnership?

Yes, infallibility.

Copies of the *APT Handbook* are currently kept under lock and key. Soon, though, it is expected that all copies of the manual will be destroyed and the training sessions will cease altogether. The three-year charter for the committee has expired and is not likely to be renewed.

A recent study conducted by the FWS Executive Committee has concluded that the quality of new partners admitted since the advent of APT is no higher than those admitted in prior years. This has confirmed the view, held by many when APT was first established, that partnership is not something one can be taught—you're either born to be a partner or you're not.

Whom to Anoint?

Decisions at FWS as to who will be admitted to partnership and who condemned forever to purgatory as an associate, who allowed to grasp the golden ring and who never
to know the firm's net income, who to bask in glory and who
to continue to be a bit actor, who to become infallible and
who to remain perpetually in need of an eraser, is entrusted
to a committee so secret that its composition is unknown
even to its members. Anonymity is preserved by requiring
committee members, except Stanley J. Fairweather and his
trusty secretary, Ms. Oxenhandle, to wear paper bags over
their heads during meetings.

Since Ms. Oxenhandle was unable to attend and take
minutes, Stanley dictated the following recollections of a
recent meeting of the Committee Regarding Admission to
Partnership:

The meeting of the CRAP Committee commenced with
the customary invocation: "O great and silent Senior
Partner in the sky, we are gathered today to consider,
inter alia, who should be admitted to our humble but
lucrative temporal partnership. We pray that you will
guide us to select only those, if any, who are truly worthy
of anointment. Let us not be swayed to pollute the purity
of our partnership by mere compassion for decent human
beings who have worked loyally and well for us for many
years. Rather, let us bless only those whose entry will
uplift our Bottom Line. Thanks a lot. Amen."

The first question for consideration was whether to
call Beverly Post-Humous to partnership. Kicking off the
discussion, Mr. A remarked that, practically speaking, he
did not see how the firm could deny Beverly partnership.
It was becoming increasingly important, he weened, as
law school enrollment of the fairer sex mushroomed, to be
able to attract top-flight women lawyers.

The firm's reputation among the ladies was not enhanced recently when separate recruiting felonies were

filed by seven major law schools based on sexist remarks allegedly made by FWS interviewers. The alleged remarks ranged from "Nice to meet you, honeybunch" to "What do we do if you get knocked up and the little bugger is due during a big trial?"

The firm's image among women was tarnished still further by the adoption of what some took to be a less than generous "parenting leave" policy, which permits either parent to take off the entire day of the child's birth, but counts it as a vacation day. Could we afford, given this history, to deny a woman associate who has toiled in the firm's vineyards for nine long years, admission to partnership? Mr. A asked rhetorically.

In partial reply, Ms. B pointed out that Beverly Post-Humous was a man.

Debate focused next on Beverly's work product. Those in the probate department lauded his work. Some typical comments were: "Does a really nifty pour-over will with marital trust" and "No better contingent charitable remainderman in the office."

With what he claimed was all due respect, Mr. C questioned how much legal talent drafting wills actually demanded, suggesting that, with all of the forms available, a gifted rodent could be trained to do probate work. One member who, it may be presumed, had close ties to the probate department, took apparent umbrage and cried.

Speaking on behalf of the bereaved, Mr. D voiced the view that even assuming, *arguendo*, that a gifted rodent could perform the task (adding, parenthetically, that in his view the rodent would have to be "near-genius level"), this did not necessarily mean that Post-Humous should be denied admission. The firm needed people who could belt out wills and codicils and hold widows' hands and, on the evidence, Beverly seemed to be able to do all of that passing well. It was further noted that no one had ever heard a client complain about Beverly's work.

"Dead men tell no tales," rebutted Mr. C.

Mr. E. questioned whether even a wizard will-person should be anointed, given that this area of practice was notoriously unprofitable.

In response, the bereaved's representative entreated the committee not to disrecollect that it was only through drafting cheap wills that the firm was privileged later to loot wealthy estates. And even if that were not true, he argued, as a full-service law firm, we should view probate as a loss leader.

Mr. C said that while he was quite prepared to accept probate as a loss leader, the question was whether the firm needed additional loss-leader partners.

Here Mr. D. interjected that Beverly had labored long and hard for the firm and had received excellent reviews, raises and bonuses. Indeed, not infrequently he had extended himself well beyond the call of duty to act as a pallbearer for important departed clients.

Ms. B allowed as how it was difficult to consider, in the abstract, whether Beverly should be admitted without knowing what the standard for partnership was. Was it competence in one's field, intellectual parity with the firm's weakest partner, an absolute standard of excellence in the law, ability to please clients, visibility in the profession or the community, possession of substantial billing responsibility, an ability to supervise and keep associates occupied, a talent at sucking up to the important partners in the firm, loyalty and longevity of service, a mystic sense of calling, a combination of the foregoing—or what?

The consensus seemed to be that it was the latter—"or what."

At this point, Mr. A recurred to the issue he had raised earlier of the firm's ability to attract female lawyers. Though admitting that he had been temporarily sidetracked by the revelation that Beverly Post-Humous was of the male persuasion, he argued that, on reflection, the thrust of his original argument had lost none of its cogency. Indeed, if *he* had not realized after nine years that Bev was a fella, how would female law students, seeing a Beverly on the letterhead, recognize that she was a he? Therefore, Mr. A argued, for the reasons advanced earlier, it seemed imperative that Beverly be admitted to partnership.

Thereupon, on motion duly made and seconded, Beverly was hoisted unanimously into the ranks of the infallible.

Howdy, Pardner

Stanley J. Fairweather looked at six paper bags around the table. Under each was the head of one of his partners. "CRAP!" Stanley thought to himself, eschewing the temptation to think to others. And he was right, CRAP it was.

In an atmosphere so tense that one could cut it with a machete, the Committee Regarding Admission to Partnership was conducting its annual meeting. So powerful was this committee that Stanley thought it prudent for members to speak through electronic sound distorters which made the speaker's voice unrecognizable. Only Stanley and his faithful secretary, Ms. Oxenhandle, knew who the CRAPers were. As usual, Ms. Oxenhandle had started the meeting ritual by inviting the members into Stanley's office one by one, bagging each of them, instructing them to hold hands (gloved) and leading them to a waiting VW minibus to be transported to the secret locus of the meeting (which actually was an FWS conference room).

This year's meeting promised to be a particularly difficult one. Last year the committee had elected only one new partner, Beverly Post-Humous. This year, the committee had four candidates to consider. Lewis Handlefull of the corporate department, Robert Grinder of the litigation department, James Francis of the tax department and Lucinda Sixshooter-Fong of the bankruptcy department. Each of them had his or her supporters and detractors.

Ms. Oxenhandle took minutes. She used code letters in place of members' names in her minutes, even though only Stanley Fairweather received a copy.

Stanley approved the minutes of the last meeting, and then Mr. E moved that the committee reject all four candidates. Such a course, he argued, would save them a tremendous amount of time. "Time is of the essence," he reminded them. (Although E wasn't sure whether that saying applied here, his old contracts professor had told him it was a good line, and to use it whenever possible.) "More importantly, though," Mr. E continued, "time is money. A penny saved is, after all, a penny earned, not to mention the interest. Therefore," he argued, "to save a lot of time would be to earn a lot of money." This, he pointed out, would be welcome, given the firm's recent financial difficulties.

Ms. B protested: "Rejecting all of the candidates summarily would be unfair to those associates who had labored long and hard on behalf of the firm and deserved to be considered for partnership. They should not be passed over merely because that would save the firm some time."

"Even assuming *arguendo* that fairness is the least bit relevant to partnership questions," replied Mr. E, "and that the other bleeding hearts on this committee will be swayed by your argument, I have another reason why none of the candidates should be made a partner—it would be a big mistake."

"How can you be so damn certain that making any of the candidates a partner would be a big mistake?" asked Mr. D.

"History," answered Mr. E. "In the last ten years we haven't had one person who was worthy of admission to partnership."

"But we've made twenty-two new partners in that time," protested Ms. B.

"That's right. Look at them," replied Mr. E.

Mr. A interrupted. It was unseemly to be talking of their partners in that way, he thought.

"It's unseemly to have partners of the sort we've admitted over the last decade," Mr. E retorted.

Stanley gave E an expulsion warning, and reminded him that truth is no defense.

"But if we don't make them all partners, they'll leave the firm," Ms. B said concernedly.

"That's blackmail," Mr. E recognized, "and I don't think we should stand for it. At least we shouldn't take it lying down. Who do the little bastards think they are, threatening to leave like that, biting the hand that feeds them, holding a gun to our heads, scaremongering, browbeating us, trying to bulldoze us into it. The only thing we have to fear is fear itself. . . ."

"Wait a minute. Nobody has threatened us," said Mr. A. "And if they're smart, they won't. Where would they go? They've priced themselves out of the market. I don't think we have to worry much about their leaving."

Mr. D said he thought it was about time CRAP got beyond the generalities and began discussing the individual candidates. He would like to speak in favor of Lewis Handlefull, of corporate. Over the last several years, Lewis had brought several significant clients to the firm. Therefore, he thought Handlefull ought to be admitted, because the firm needed partners who could bring in business.

Mr. C objected, saying that bringing in new business was but one consideration for partnership. Handlefull, he said, was a terrible namedropper and a lackluster lawyer. He did not think that we should be admitting that sort to partnership. The firm had plenty of them as it was. James Francis, of tax, on the other hand, was a lawyer's lawyer. He knew the Internal Revenue Code practically by heart. He knew every angle, and how to play it.

"Francis might well know every angle in the tax code," said Ms. B, "but talking to him is as interesting as reading the tax code, except that the code has a better sense of humor. With clients, Francis is about the worst lawyer I've seen. And if you look around at some of our partnership meetings, you know I've seen some doozies. Just because somebody's a good technician doesn't mean that he should be made a partner."

On the other hand, Ms. B. felt that Robert Grinder was deserving of elevation to partnership. "Grinder's one of the hardest working associates the firm has. Maybe he's not the smartest person in the firm, but he isn't all that stupid. Though he hasn't brought in any clients to speak of, he hasn't lost many, either. Grinder's a pretty decent all-around lawyer."

"Mediocrity," cried Mr. C. "All you have to do is listen

to that description. It reeks of mediocrity. Partnership ought to be an achievement. Not everybody can make it. Many are called, few are chosen. Just because we've got twenty or thirty Grinders, we don't have to take in another one. If we're going to make one a partner, it might as well be Lucinda Sixshooter-Fong. She, at least, would do us some good, being 20 percent American Indian, 20 percent Oriental, 20 percent black, 20 percent WASP, and 20 percent female."

Ms. B reminded C that, though FWS was an equal opportunity partnership, the firm did not admit somebody to partnership just because of race, origin, sex or creed.

"Yaah, I know," replied Mr. C, "but what about all four?"

"What if we compromise and take all of them in?" asked Mr. A.

"That way we won't have the associate unrest that we always get when we accept some but not all of the people who are up for partnership."

"We're not running this firm to avoid associate unrest, damnit," reasoned Mr. E, "although at times it's a little hard to prove that from the way we behave. If we're going to let them control all of our decisions, why not make them the partners and we can be the associates?"

"Hey, I like that idea," piped Ms. B. "It's kinda like that Associate-Partner Day we had before the Morale Committee was disbanded."

"He was kidding, you dodo," explained C.

"Even if we wanted to make all of them partners," said Mr. E, "we couldn't afford to do it. There's only 100 percent of the profits to split, and every bit of it is spoken for."

"That's it!" said Ms. B excitedly. "We tell them that we really wanted to make them partners, but we checked and found that all 100 percent of the profits had been allocated. That way they know that the decision was out of our hands."

"Wait a minute," said Stanley Fairweather. "That

dumb suggestion just gave me an idea. We keep thinking about making partners as though it were just a matter of percentages and profits."

"What other way is there?" asked Ms. B.

"My hunch is that it isn't really the profits that make associates so uptight about not making partner. It's what failing to make partner says to the rest of the world about their abilities. If they're not made partners, they think everybody will assume it was because they didn't have the legal ability.

"So, if we just give them big offices and call them partners, we won't have to worry about splitting the profits with them at all."

"But Stanley," said Ms. B, "our partnership agreement provides that all partners share in the profits. So how can we make them partners without having them share?"

"Easy, we make them pardners, not partners. We amend the partnership agreement to say that a pardner is an associate with a large office. To the outside world, they're partners; to us, they're just our pardners."

And the meeting ended with Stanley leading a joyous, albeit distorted, rendition of "Home, Home on the Range."

The Ballad of Nails Nuttree

Every law firm has its legends, and Seymour "Nails" Nuttree certainly qualifies as one at Fairweather, Winters & Sommers.

Nails litigates. In fact, Nails heads the FWS litigation department. Nobody else at FWS litigates like Nails, a statement to which most associates would append "fortunately." A recent case shows pretty well how Nails runs the FWS litigation department.

Roundup International Ltd., one of FWS's blue-chip New York Stock Exchange clients, was slapped with a complaint by the Environmental Protection Agency charging, in separate counts, air pollution, water pollution, noise pollution, toxic waste generation and failure to yield the right of way to passing deer. The call from RIL came to Stanley Fairweather, since Stanley sits on the RIL Board of Directors by virtue of his legal acumen and the happy marriage of his daughter, Becky, to RIL's chief executive officer, Robert "Last" Roundup (so nicknamed because of certain permanent birth control measures taken by Last's parents after the unexpected arrival of their ninth child, Robert).

Stanley immediately dispatched one of FWS's wing-footed messengers to the RIL offices to bring back a copy of the complaint. While awaiting the messenger's return, Stanley roughed out some figures on his "Sayings from Stanley" memo pad. The numbers 3,400 and $16.4 billion were impressive, representing estimates of the maximum prison term and damages, respectively, that could arise from government success in the suit. Clearly, this was one for Nails.

Stanley called Nails, explaining the situation briefly and suggesting that Nails stop 'round at Stanley's office. Glancing at his Dan Quayle wristwatch, and seeing the little hand on four and the big hand approaching twelve, Nails asked Stanley to give him ten minutes to make a few phone calls.

Nails' first call was to the chief receptionist, instructing her to advise the other sentinels not to allow any associate to leave the office. Next he phoned the office manager to tell her he'd need six secretaries and two word-processing operators to stay the night. He rang the head of the messenger staff to have him send a crew to the RIL offices to begin to move all RIL files over to FWS, instructing that they be brought directly to the FWS duplicating department, where four copies of everything should be made. Nails' next call was to Hiring Committee Chairman Rex Gladhand, to alert him to the fact that he would need eight non-partnership-track bodies to work on "something big." Then he buzzed his secretary demanding that, ASAP, she instruct the paralegal coordinator to set aside five paralegals for the case, the conference room reservationist to book two large and one small conference rooms for the next four years, and the housekeeping personnel to set up dinner for thirty that evening. This was what had come to be known around the firm as Nails' Red Alert.

Nails walked into Stanley's office, uttered a gruff "How're you," and plunked himself down in the soft chair across the desk from Stanley's. "Whadda ya think?" asked Nails.

"What do you think, Nails?" asked Stanley, neatly turning the question back on his ace litigator.

"I think this is one we'd better treat seriously." Though Nails' understatement had not been intended as humorous, he acknowledged his witticism when Stanley chuckled in agreement.

"Who do you think ought to handle it, Nails?"

"I'm not sure, Stan, but I think it's crucial we get the right team on this one, and the ticket is big enough that it'll bear whatever freight it takes to get that team. My thought is to try something new.

"The way I see it, we give each of our litigating partners a copy of the complaint, tell 'em we haven't decided who should try the case yet and ask each to pick three associates and a paralegal. We then divide them into plaintiff and defendant teams and have them prepare briefs and argue the case. Our Continuing Legal Advancement Program brief-writing instructor will grade the briefs and a panel of our three retired judge-partners will score the oral arguments. This process should not only find our best team, but get a substantial amount of research done, expose us to the other side's strongest arguments and produce some not insignificant legal fees."

"I like it, Nails. We'll call it the Fairweather Moot Court Competition."

The competition, run by Stanley J. Fairweather, the surprise choice as the first Fairweather Moot Court Board Chairman, was a rousing success, though at times the competition got a bit ugly. As brief due dates approached, many key cases and articles were sliced out of their volumes by competitive, former law review associates.

All rancor was forgotten, though, after the impressive final oral arguments, held in the Stanley J. Fairweather Courtroom and attended by the entire firm. The initial unhappiness of the non-legal staff at having to give up their cafeteria and a portion of the non-legal ladies' room to make space for the courtroom was lost in the splendor of the Himalayan Cedar paneling and in the firing of the three primary complainers. The Fairweather Moot Court Loving Cup, inscribed with the names of the winning team, is housed in a handsome cabinet outside the courtroom.

United States v. Roundup progressed at a crawl. Initial settlement discussions with the government bogged down first over the shape of the conference room table, then over a series of other matters of lesser import.

Seeing no alternative but to assume the matter was going to trial, Nails designated one of the conference rooms as the War Room and pitched tent. He ordered twenty legal-size bunkbeds to cradle his troops and lined the corridors with them. The seven associates who quit in protest of the working conditions were quickly replaced by the Hiring Committee in response to Nails' requisition for seven new bodies.

Meanwhile, another conference room was designated Computer Central and six Cobol experts were hired to code information from all of the RIL documents and feed them into the Tandem 600 purchased for the occasion. The computer also received the coded information from material produced by the government in response to Nails' twice-daily document requests.

Gerald "Dilly" Forspiel, newly nicknamed for his expertise in dilatory trial tactics, assembled a crew to produce motions to quash, dismiss, make the complaint more definite, disqualify counsel, have the trial judge recuse himself, and change venue. Though his Motion to Dismiss on General Principles of Offensive Practice, arguing the government's approach was so nasty and distasteful that the case should be dismissed, failed, it won Dilly high marks for creativity and attracted considerable law review comment; see, e.g., Fairweather, "Motion to DOG-POOP: Sound Litigation Strategy or a Bunch of Crap," 82 *Harv. L. Rev.* 482 (1989).

Depositions were scheduled and taken from coast to coast. Reams of paper were xeroxed in response to document requests. Motions were made, argued, briefed and decided. Millions in Roundup legal fees coated the FWS coffers. And the first Roundup partner, an associate who had spent his entire career at FWS working only on *U.S. v. Roundup*, was beknighted.

The case, meanwhile, inched its way toward trial. Nails ordered the litigation department dietician to switch the in-court team to raw meat in preparation for the ensuing battle. The calm before the storm set in.

But shortly before the scheduled trial, the American presidential election took place. The Republican candidate, to whom Last and his family had contributed a biblical fortieth portion of their combined wealth, emerged victorious. And since one of the new president's platform planks was "Stop picking on the wealthy," it was no surprise when *U.S. v. Roundup* was dismissed on the government's own motion.

Nails notched another victory on his belt, assuring that his legend would continue to haunt the next generation of FWS associates.

Slicing the Partnership Pie

The biannual Fairweather, Winters & Sommers partnership meeting to slice the partnership pie took place last Monday evening in the conference room constructed especially for that purpose. The room contains no windows and boasts nicely padded walls, and everything in the room that weighs more than fourteen ounces is bolted down. Members of the firm are frisked for weapons on their way into the room, and no sharp objects are allowed in the meeting. Pizza and beer were shuttled in from Pizzeria Uno.

In Stanley Fairweather's absence, Oscar Winters refereed.

Winters offered some opening remarks. "You all know why we are here tonight. I hope and trust that this meeting will be conducted with the dignity appropriate to a group such as ours. I remind you that we are all professionals, and the type of nastiness, swearing and violence that has characterized our past pie-slicing meetings will no longer be tolerated. To that end, we have engaged four members of the Strongarm Security Company to act as co-sergeants-at-arms for the meeting. They have assured me that the Doberman pinschers you see here are totally harmless if you behave yourselves, and will attack only if directed to do so by one of the Strongarm guards. The dogs and guards have both been advised not to eat anything offered to them by partners and have been appraised of the unfortunate guard poisoning that occurred at the last pie-slicing meeting, the report of which did not play well for us in *The All-American Lawyer*. Now, when the bell rings, I'd like to see good clean discussion. Good luck to you all, and may the best partners emerge rich. Are there any questions? . . . Yes, Manley?"

"Will there be a warning before the Dobermans actually attack anyone?"

"I'm hoping sincerely that no attack will be necessary, but in the event that one is, the Chair reserves the right to call on the dogs without warning in the event of a particularly egregious breach of etiquette. Now, if there are no further questions, let's get under way."

"I would like to suggest that we simplify the matter and end the meeting quickly by simply extending the percentages now in effect for another two years," offered Harvey Holdem.

"Well, that certainly is a simple suggestion, sorta what one would expect from a simpleton like you, Harvey," said Hector Morgan.

"I'm going to give you a warning, Hector. Please try to remember that you are dealing with partners of yours and, even if some of them are simpletons, it serves no purpose to say so," cautioned the Chair.

One of the other partners pointed out to Harvey that some of the partners had been more productive in the past two years and that some upward percentage adjustment would seem to be appropriate. Harvey said that he had no objection to an upward adjustment for those people, so long as it could be done without adversely affecting the percentages of the other partners. One of the other partners took Harvey quietly aside, and the flow of the meeting continued.

Beverly Post-Humous, newcomer to the partnership, piped up, "I think we could all save a lot of time if we would just agree to split up the pie equally. After all, as one of my favorite cases in law school held, 'We are all equal before the law.' Besides, even if one of us gets a little bit of an advantage for a couple of months, it will all come out in the wash."

"Beverly, we all may be equal *before* the law, but not *in* the law. And you're one of those who is a little bit less equal, so you'd better get used to it. As to it all coming out in the wash eventually, you might be right, but we operate on a two-year wash cycle, so why don't you just go and spin dry." Ruth Tender generally called 'em like they were.

Beverly cried. The Chair cast a disapproving look at Ruth. And the meeting went on.

Stephen Falderall suggested that it might help the meeting to reach a decision if the partners attempted to isolate and agree on the factors that ought to be considered in determining the partnership shares. While several people voiced the view that the exercise would not help at all, they were overruled.

In the course of the discussion of relevant factors which took place over the ensuing three hours, the following were suggested as pertinent: length of service with the firm, hours billed, clients controlled, associates occupied with work, neatness, pro bono work performed, height, bar association work, club memberships, number of children in college, type of work done, committee work performed in the firm, congeniality, number of friends on the Executive Committee, quality of work performed and demeanor. In an effort to give some weight to the factors, Jane Hokum-Cohen suggested that each partner rate the factors in the order of importance, assigning 10 points to the most important factor, 9 to the next most important factor and so on and so forth.

Two members of FWS's certified public accounting firm were called over to collect the ballots and to act as tellers of election. While the ballots were being counted, the Chair suggested that each of the partners put his or her head on the conference table to take a little rest. After some twenty minutes, the accountants reentered the room and announced that they had come out exactly even, except that one ballot had had to be voided because each of the items had been marked with either a 10 or a 9. Herb Gander said that was what he thought "and so forth and so on" had meant.

Stephan Mestrow said that he was getting "pretty bleeping fed up with this whole process" and was not going to kill the entire evening like this. One of the Dobermans barked, but was quieted when a guard commanded, "No, Pinky, sit; it's not time for Pinky to kill—yet."

Sherman Clayton, formerly chair of the firm's antitrust department (when there was antitrust work) and also formerly chair of the mergers and acquisitions department (when there was M & A work) and now chair of the bankruptcy department, said that he thought the partners in his current department deserved at least 25 percent increases in their percentages because of the enormous amount of billings that they had produced that year.

He noted that in recent years quite a number of small specialty firms had sprung up around the city, some of them the offshoots of much larger firms.

Percifal Snikkety said that he viewed this as a thinly-veiled threat and that he resented it. Clayton denied that he was making any threat and resented the insinuation by Snikkety that he was making a threat. Snikkety said that he resented Clayton insulting the intelligence of the partners at the meeting (with certain exceptions, whom he declined to name) by pretending that he was not making a threat. The Chair asked the guards to ready the dogs for possible attack.

Gary Swath suggested that, as long as the accountants were still there, each of the partners should write down a suggested percentage interest for each of the other partners and give those numbers to the accountants. The accountants could total and average the results and the percentages derived could be used for the next two years. The Chair ruled Swath's idea out of order as stupid.

Ruth Tender asked whether it wouldn't be appropriate to adjourn the meeting, since they didn't seem to be getting anywhere and because, since Stanley Fairweather was not there, no decision could be reached in any event.

James Sommers said that he had almost forgotten, but Stanley had given him a little note to give to the Chair, which James now handed to the Chair. Oscar opened the envelope, glanced at the paper and announced that Stanley had thoughtfully given the meeting his recommendations on what the split of the pie should be. The recommendations were passed around and the Chair asked whether there were any serious objections to the recommendations because, otherwise, he would assume that they were acceptable. There being no objections, serious or otherwise, the pie was declared split for another two years.

And the Dobermans polished off the remaining pizza and beer.

The Nominations Are Closed

Following are the minutes of the Election Committee, created to implement the new Fairweather, Winter, & Sommers policy of electing its Executive Committee.

Committee Chair Ellen Jane Ritton called the meeting to order. The Chair asked Ms. Oxenhandle to serve as secretary. This being the first meeting of the committee, it was agreed, unanimously, to dispense with reading the minutes of the last meeting.

The Chair asked that the committee first address the issue of how candidates for the Executive Committee should be nominated. Franklin "Goody" Goodtime recommended that nomination be done through party convention. Dolly Fu Lish pointed out that there were no parties in the firm, excepting, of course, the summer outing and the firm Christmas party. Goodtime admitted that this was true, but noted that many of the partners were members of one of the two major political parties, and that those parties provided a model the firm might use for its nominations. Dolly argued that the process of state primaries and caucuses was too laborious and costly a process for the firm's purposes. Besides, painful memories of the 1968 Democratic Convention would be evoked for several members of the Pro Bono Publico Committee.

F. Frederick Feedrop said that, speaking of cost, he was interested in what sort of campaign finance restrictions ought to be imposed on candidates for the Executive Committee. He proposed that no person be allowed to contribute more than $5000 to any candidate, and that the list of each candidate's contributions be published in the office bulletin, weekly. Dolly pointed out that the office bulletin is published only bi-weekly. Fred said that that explained why he hadn't seen more issues lately.

[At this point, Ms. Oxenhandle decided to switch to reporting the exact words of the speakers, or as close as she could come, given that she hasn't taken much dictation from Mr. Fairweather lately, with him away so much on business in the firm's Grand Cayman Island branch, so her shorthand may be a bit rusty.]

"This discussion is getting too far afield," said Ellen Jane. "I don't imagine that we're going to have open campaigning, so all of this campaign finance stuff is irrelevant. Let's try to get a bit more practical."

"I don't see why we need any nominations," argued Sheldon Horvitz. "Why can't we just all vote?"

"It'll be a one to one to one, etc. tie," predicted Fred.

"Well, okay then, we could just have nominations at a firm meeting," said Sheldon.

"You mean just, well, open and notorious?" asked Fred.

"Of course, why not?" Sheldon replied.

"Right to privacy and fifth amendment," said Fred.

"If you're that uptight about it, we could try it by secret nomination," said Sheldon.

"Now you're talking," said Fred.

"Should we put any restrictions on who can be nominated?" asked Dolly.

"No, I think partners ought to be able to select whoever they want, regardless of sex," said Geodfrey Bleschieu.

"I wasn't talking about sex. I mean, for instance, should a person have to have been a partner for a certain period of time before serving on the E.C.?"

"Are we limiting the E.C. to partners?" Sheldon asked.

"Are you suggesting that you'd let *associates* serve on the Executive Committee?" asked Ellen Jane, incredulous.

"Why not, there are twice as many of them as there are of us, and those who stay will be around the firm a lot longer than we will. Why shouldn't their views be represented?" Sheldon replied.

"It would be a hell of an advantage in recruiting law students," added Geodfrey.

"You two must be out of your minds. If we came up with a rule allowing associates to be elected to the E.C., we'd be drummed out of the firm," said Ellen Jane.

"I agree," said Dolly, "but what about limitations as to the number of years somebody's been a partner?"

"Are you talking maximum or minimum?" asked Sheldon.

"You know very well what I mean," said Dolly.

"I don't see any reason to limit it," said Geodfrey. "If we want to elect somebody who's just been made a partner, why not? But we need some way of assuring that the different areas of our practice are represented."

"Yes, that's very important," agreed Ellen Jane. "We've been lucky in the past to have had a good balance."

"That's not luck, that's Stanley," said Dolly.

"What do you mean?" asked Fred.

"Well, in the past, Stanley Fairweather chose the E.C. He made sure that we had representation from all departments—different personalities, points of view," Dolly explained.

"He sure did a great job," mused Sheldon.

"Well, then why don't we let him continue?" asked Fred.

"Because the firm has decided that we should *elect* our Executive Committee, and we were created to tell them how," answered Ellen Jane.

Suddenly the writer, Ms. Oxenhandle, me, who had been silent throughout (because she was busy taking notes) spoke up, "If you'll forgive me for interrupting, I have a suggestion: I think Mr. Fairweather might be persuaded by you to make the *nominations*. Then the whole partnership could vote to elect the nominees. That would solve all of your problems as to qualifications, balance— and everything else. And it will assure we get a good E.C., to boot."

The rest of the committee, recognizing the obvious

merit and simplicity of my suggestion, agreed unanimously. And the Election Committee meeting was adjourned, *sine die.*

Ebbing the Partnership Flow

For decades, the Fairweather, Winters & Sommers Executive Committee had assumed that associates were the root of all firm problems. First came the problem of hiring them, then of evaluating them, then of trying to retain or fire them and, finally, of determining whether to make them partners. Once they became partners, all problems vanished.

In recent months, though, FWS was experiencing a new phenomenon: partners were beginning to leave the firm. Some left in droves, taking substantial chunks of business. Others dribbled out: some to teach law school, some to pursue other forms of retirement. Unsure what to make of the departures, the Executive Committee charged an Ad Hoc Committee on Partnership Retention with determining the reason for the outflow of partners and making recommendations on how to ebb the flow. Below is an account of the last meeting of the ad hoc committee.

Chairman Harry Ratchet summoned the meeting to order. Ratchet announced that committee member Otto Flack would be unable to attend, since he had left the firm yesterday to apprentice himself to a pest exterminator. The firm would be throwing a going away party for Otto tomorrow and had purchased a six-foot-high monogrammed fly swatter as a gag gift. Ratchet tossed the floor open to suggestions on how to curb further partner outflow.

"To my mind," offered Hector Morgan, "partners are leaving because of a lack of security."

Stephan Mestrow disagreed vehemently with Morgan. "Being a partner at Fairweather, Winters & Sommers is one of the most secure positions a person could have.

We've been in existence over forty years now and we're likely to be around for another forty."

"My meaning has eluded you, Stephan m' boy. I mean that it's simply too easy for a partner to pick up and leave the firm," replied Hector. "I propose that the firm establish a new policy. Partners should be permitted to leave the office only for compelling reasons, and only upon furnishing reasonable security that they will return."

Lydia Milife thought Morgan's suggestion might run afoul of whichever amendment to the U.S. Constitution it was—in the teens somewhere, as she recalled—that prohibited involuntary servitude.

Vance "Rip" Winkle disagreed. The Thirteenth Amendment had not been intended to prohibit partners from being held captive in a law firm. To buttress his argument, Winkle launched into a capsule history of the post-Civil War era, surfacing briefly for air at Grover Cleveland.

Mestrow ventured that, even if Morgan's suggestion did not run afoul of the Constitution, it presented more serious problems. For one thing, it would apply to everyone sitting in the room. Stephan did not relish the notion of captivity, however posh and comfy the firm's offices might be. Besides, the Finance Committee would flip at the cost of maintaining a security force sufficient to keep tabs on partners who might try to escape. Furthermore, when word of the new security policy leaked to law schools, it would adversely affect the firm's already tenuous ability to recruit new lawyers.

Lydia suggested amending the firm partnership agreement to prohibit partners from leaving. Mestrow, though, feared that such a provision would violate the antitrust statutes and might not be enforceable even at common law, since it would effectively prohibit partners from practicing their profession.

"Instead of actually prohibiting a partner from leaving," suggested Morgan, "we could establish a financial penalty for withdrawing from the firm that would make leaving less desirable."

"That'll never work, Hector," Rachel Steinberg opined. "If the financial penalty is too small, it won't scare anyone. And if it's too high it won't work, since all of us partners are judgment proof, anyway."

"Maybe we're putting the plough before the tractor by considering methods of preventing partners from leaving without first trying to identify their reasons for leaving," Chairman Ratchet suggested. "Since we've got a considerable pool of former partners who are now experts on the subject, why not contact them and ask them why they left?"

"Are you kidding? Most of our departed partners are our fierce competitors. Do you think they'll answer why they left candidly? And how the hell do you suggest we reach Swami Pungah?[1] And Tony Holland was virtually incomprehensible while he was at the firm. I doubt his new position as professor of legal history at Hammurabi School of Law has honed his communication skills any."

Rachel argued that the committee's inability to discover the real reasons why partners had left needn't disturb them. They could posit their own reasons, which would probably prove more interesting than the real reasons, anyway. They might start, she suggested, by examining the reasons associates typically give for leaving, to see whether those apply to partners as well.

On examination, the committee determined that the associates' reasons did not seem to apply to partners. Partners who had left were well compensated. So it could not have been salary. Since each departee had his own secretary, none could complain of inadequate support. And a review of the departees' billable hours revealed that they lagged well behind the firm, city, state and nation-

---

1 Editor's Note: The former Irving Helperin, an ex-FWS partner who had taken up residence on a mountain top in the Bengali region of India.

wide averages. Finally, since all of them were already partners, it could not be the fear of being passed over that had prompted them to leave.

The committee appeared to have butted up against a brick wall, when Rip perked up and signaled the arrival of an idea, "Ooh, ooh, ooh, I've got an idea. Maybe partners leaving isn't a problem at all. We were running short of partner-sized offices, and the departures will make plenty of them available. That should be attractive to senior associates."

"And," Lydia chimed in, "the departures will create gaps in our legal expertise that will present many associates with excellent partnership opportunities."

"Partners leaving might even be a boon to those of us who remain partners," Rachel opined. "There'll be a lot more partnership percentage to pass around."

"That's true," noted Morgan, "but unfortunately the partners who left accounted for roughly fifty percent of the revenue to which our partnership percentage is applied."

The mood of the meeting darkened perceptibly at Morgan's observation, until Chairman Ratchet interrupted the gloom, "I bet I know why partners are leaving. They're lacking a sense that they are doing a good job."

"What d'ya mean by that?" asked Rachel.

"Well, associates who do a good job are told so regularly," said Ratchet. "Clients tell them and the firm tells them at least twice a year, at their salary and bonus reviews. But do clients tell a partner that he did a good job? Hell no. All they do is complain about the bill. And partners don't have periodic reviews at which the firm heaps praise on them. We admit people to partnership and that's it. No more 'Nice job, Harry,' or 'Attagirl, Lucy.' They're supposed to feel that they've made it. But they have no goals left. They're too secure. I think we should establish a policy of reviewing and evaluating partners for continuing partnership. That will give partners something to aspire to, and something to worry a bit about."

"By Jove, I think you're right!" exclaimed Hector. "I told you the problem was security."

The ad hoc committee embraced Chairman Ratchet's suggestion unanimously. And the Executive Committee was so pleased with the ad hoc committee's work that it constituted it the Standing Committee on Partnership Evaluation.

Off with His Head

Tension ran high in the FWS Executive Committee. Never before had they considered the expulsion of a Fairweather, Winters & Sommers partner. Not formally anyway. Informally, they discussed it, on average, six times a day.

"What if we discuss this in code?" suggested Seymour "Nails" Nuttree. "If we refer to you-know-who as, say, Donald Duck, wouldn't that take care of it?"

"Are you nuts? What if somebody overheard that. The Fairweather Executive Committee talking about the expulsion of Donald Duck!" countered Acting Chair Sherman Clayton.

"You've got a point."

"Hey, we could mime it," offered Nails.

"Super idea, charades," said the Chair. "Why don't we just pick teams, too?"

"Well, we'd better forget it, then," said Nails. "I don't see how we can risk that some of you-know-who will find out."

"That's the most ridiculous thing I've ever heard in my life," shouted Phillip D.W. Wilson III. "We've got a partner we're thinking of canning and we can't do it because we're afraid someone might overhear our discussion!"

"Sssh, for Godsake!" whispered Harry Punctillio.

"Look, our problem is we're sitting around this big conference table, which is pretty close to the door, and we've got to talk loud in order to hear one another. If we all move our chairs over there, into the corner of the room farthest from the door, and talk quietly, we should be okay," suggested Sue Pritchet.

The meeting recessed for five minutes while the partners moved their chairs over to the corner of the conference room. When the group reconvened, Stephen announced that, unfortunately, he and Harry had run into Lance Byte while moving a coffee table into the conference room.

"But luckily," Falderall told the group, "Harry had his wits about him."

"What did you say, Harry?" asked the Chair.

"I told Lance that you had sprained your ankle and needed to elevate it on the coffee table. So you're going to have to walk around with a limp for awhile."

"Did he ask how I sprained it?"

"As a matter of fact, he did. I told him you climbed up on the conference table to change the fluorescent light and twisted your ankle when you stepped on a coffee cup."

"You didn't tell him that?!"

"Well, it's not easy to come up with a quick way of spraining somebody's ankle in an Executive Committee meeting. You try it some time."

"We'd better break a coffee cup then, if I supposedly stepped on one."

"Good thinking. You'd make a great criminal."

"Never mind. Here, I'll break it. There. Damn, why didn't you tell me there was coffee in it? Did you say which ankle, by the way?"

"No, but there was one other thing. Lance offered to come in with some ice, but I told him that Sue had already put an Ace bandage on, so one of us had better run down to the drug store to pick one up so you can wrap your ankle."

The meeting broke for another fifteen minutes to allow time to purchase the bandage and wrap the Chair's ankle. The Chair did not find Phillip's purchase of a get-well card humorous, but his opinion was in a distinct minority.

Finally, the meeting turned to a discussion of the expulsion. "Phillip, you're the one who raised this in the first place. Why do you think we ought to expel Herb?"

"Herb? I was talking about Fred!"

"I thought it was Alex!"

"We can take others up later if you like, but I think it's just gotten out of hand with Fred. I mean, it's embarrassing. Last week he had our client sign ten original notes at a closing, so everyone would have one for his records. If Jane Dereks, our second-year associate, hadn't been there to take Fred aside, our client would have been half a million dollars in debt on a fifty-thousand-dollar loan."

"That's pretty bad, all right," said Sherman.

"Could happen to anybody," objected Falderall. "He just got a little carried away with closing spirit, that's all."

"Well, that's not the only thing he's done," Phillip continued. "He's ruining our reputation at the law schools. You heard what he did when he went to interview last month, didn't you?"

"No, what happened?"

"The placement director introduced him to the new woman dean of the law school and Fred called her 'cupcake.' "

"No, he didn't do that!"

"I wish I were kidding."

"Well, that's easy though. We just won't let him interview."

"Frankly, I don't understand your tolerance, but this will clinch it. You know our longtime client, Precision Tool Company, one of Stanley Fairweather's clients, matter of fact. Fred did a simple lease for them and charged them $50,000!"

"What did they do?"

"What do you think they did? They called Stanley and raised holy hell!"

"So what did Stanley do?"

"Told me he sliced the bill in half and the client was happy as a clam, even though it came to $400 an hour for Fred's time, sliced. First time the client's expressed any appreciation in twenty years, Stanley said. He's thinking of billing them that way all the time."

"I don't believe this. We've got a partner who in the last two months has shown us that he's incompetent, sexist, a menace to our recruitment efforts, and somebody who grossly overbills important clients—and we're not going to recommend that the partnership expel him?!"

"Calm down, Phillip. This thing's a balancing act. When you think about it, how much harm can one rotten partner do? But if the firm gets a reputation for expelling partners, we're dead. The fact that we've even considered it must never get beyond us six."

Just then, there was a knock on the door and the Chair called, "Come in."

"Oh, sorry, didn't know you were in a meeting. How come you're all sittin' over there?" asked Frieda, one of the paralegals who had come in for a meeting with the Chair on one of his bankruptcy cases.

"Ah, there was a draft over the conference table, so we decided to move over here," answered Harry.

"Want me to call a maintenance man for you?" asked Frieda.

"No, thank you, we're just fine, but thanks anyway."

"Okay, if you change your mind, I'm at extension 7942. Say, did you guys decide whether to give old Fred the boot yet?"

Concluding Note

Some suppose a lawyer's life dull and humorless. But those who think this lack a sense of the absurd. We lawyers are creatures (ofttimes prisoners) of our training. And large law firms are the *reductio ad absurdum* of that process.

The casual reader of these pages might emerge thinking that I regret my life at the Bar. Nothing could be farther from the truth. For all their foibles (perhaps because of them) I love my partners and my associates—and my law firm with all of its inefficient committees. I would not trade my years with them, for anything.

Actually, that's not quite true. I would trade it all to play shortstop for the Chicago Cubs. And I'm going to do that, next time around. Really. I've written it into my will. And the head of our trusts and estates department informs me that such a provision has never been held invalid.